Naomi's
GIFT

Also by Amy Clipston

A Plain and Simple Christmas

A Gift of Grace

A Promise of Hope

A Place of Peace

Young Adult

Roadside Assistance

An Amish Christmas Story

Naomi's
GIFT *a novella*

Amy Clipston

ZONDERVAN®

ZONDERVAN.com/
AUTHORTRACKER
follow your favorite authors

ZONDERVAN

Naomi's Gift
Copyright © 2011 by Amy Clipston

This title is also available as a Zondervan ebook.
Visit www.zondervan.com/ebooks.

This title is also available in a Zondervan audio edition.
Visit www.zondervan.fm.

Requests for information should be addressed to:

Zondervan, *Grand Rapids, Michigan 49530*

Library of Congress Cataloging-in-Publication Data

Clipston, Amy.
        Naomi's gift : an Amish Christmas story / Amy Clipston.
            p. cm.
        ISBN 978-0-310-32735-6 (hardcover, jacketed)
        1. Amish — Fiction. 2. Single women — Fiction. 3. Widowers — Fiction.
    4. Christmas stories. I. Title.
    PS3603.L58N36 2011
    813'.6 — dc22   2011020589

All Scripture quotations, unless otherwise indicated, are taken from The Holy Bible,
New International Version®, NIV®. Copyright © 1973, 1978, 1984 by Biblica, Inc.™ Used
by permission. All rights reserved worldwide.

Any Internet addresses (websites, blogs, etc.) and telephone numbers in this book are
offered as a resource. They are not intended in any way to be or imply an endorse-
ment by Zondervan, nor does Zondervan vouch for the content of these sites and
numbers for the life of this book.

Cover design: ThinkPen Design, Inc.
Cover photography: Shutterstock®
Interior photography: Shutterstock®
Interior design: Beth Shagene, Melissa Elenbaas

Printed in the United States of America

11 12 13 14 15 16 /DCI/ 21 20 19 18 17 16 15 14 13 12 11 10 9 8 7 6 5 4 3 2 1

For Lauran

Glossary

ach— oh
aenti — aunt
appeditlich — delicious
Ausbund — Amish hymnal with only printed words
bedauerlich — sad
boppli — baby
bruder — brother
daed — father
danki — thank you
dat — dad/daddy
dochder — daughter
Englisher — a non-Amish person
fraa — wife
Frehlicher Grischtdaag! — Merry Christmas!
freind — friend
freinden — friends
froh — happy
gegisch — silly
gern gschehne — you're welcome
grossdaddi — grandfather
Grischtdaag — Christmas
grossmammi — grandmother
gut — good
gut nacht — goodnight
Ich liebe dich — I love you

kapp — prayer covering or cap
kind — child
kinner — children
kumm — come
liewe — love, a term of endearment
maedel — young woman
mamm — mom
mei — my
mutter — mother
naerfich — nervous
narrisch — crazy
onkel — uncle
schee — pretty
schtupp — family room
schweschder — sister
Was iss letz? — What's wrong?
Wie geht's? — How do you do? or Good day!
wunderbaar — wonderful
ya — yes

Families in *Naomi's Gift*

(boldface are parents)

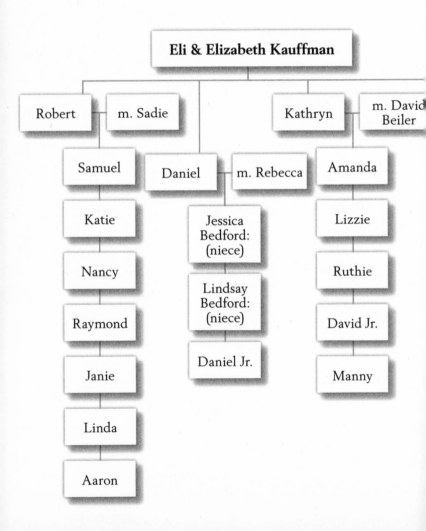

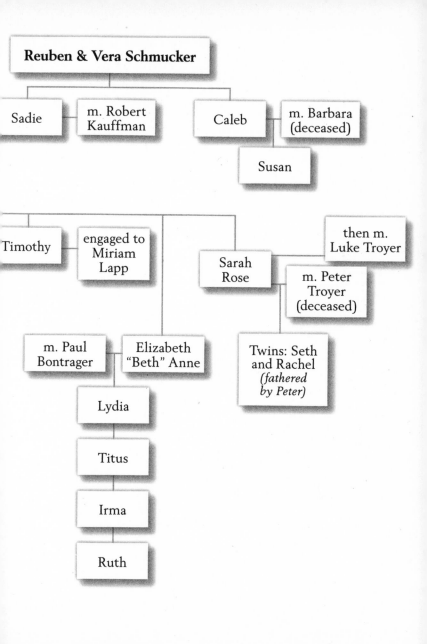

Reuben & Vera Schmucker

Sadie — m. Robert Kauffman

Caleb — m. Barbara (deceased)

Susan

Timothy — engaged to Miriam Lapp

Sarah Rose — then m. Luke Troyer

m. Peter Troyer (deceased)

m. Paul Bontrager — Elizabeth "Beth" Anne

Twins: Seth and Rachel *(fathered by Peter)*

Lydia

Titus

Irma

Ruth

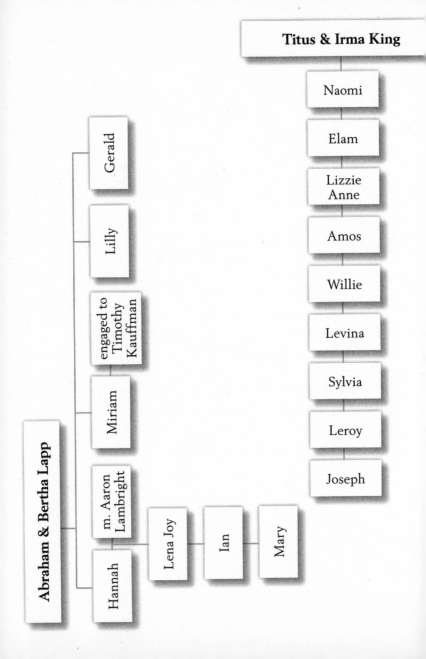

Titus & Irma King

Naomi

Elam

Lizzie Anne

Amos

Willie

Levina

Sylvia

Leroy

Joseph

Abraham & Bertha Lapp

Gerald

Lilly

engaged to Timothy Kauffman

Miriam

m. Aaron Lambright

Hannah

Lena Joy

Ian

Mary

Note to the Reader

While this novel is set against the real backdrop of Lancaster County, Pennsylvania, the characters are fictional. There is no intended resemblance between the characters in this book and any real members of the Amish and Mennonite communities. As with any work of fiction, I've taken license in some areas of research as a means to create the necessary circumstances for my characters. My research was thorough; however, it would be impossible to be completely accurate in details and description, since each and every community differs. Therefore, any inaccuracies in the Amish and Mennonite lifestyles portrayed in this book are completely due to fictional license.

CHAPTER 1

Caleb sucked in a deep breath as the taxi van bounced down Route 340 toward Bird-in-Hand, Pennsylvania. After nearly a decade, he'd returned to the town of his birth. He clasped his hands together. Why was he nervous? This was supposed to be a happy reunion with his family, and yet, his palms were sweaty with anticipation despite the biting December wind.

"*Dat!*" Susie said, grabbing the sleeve of his coat and yanking with one hand while pointing toward the indoor farmers market with the other hand. "*Dat!* Can we stop there? Can we? Please? Please?"

"Why would we stop there?" he asked. "We have a farmers market back home that's much the same."

She blew out an exasperated sigh and glowered with annoyance. "To get a gift for *Aenti* Sadie, of course. Teacher Linda says that you should always bring a nice dessert to dinner. Please, *Dat?* I'll pick something out fast like we do at the market at home." She batted her eyelashes and gave her prettiest and cutest smile. "Pretty please, *Dat?*" She looked like a mirror of her beautiful mother, and his heart turned over in his chest. At the tender age of eight, Caleb Schmucker's daughter already knew how to wrap him around her little finger.

He gave a sigh of defeat, and Susie clapped her hands while grinning with triumph.

"Driver?" Caleb asked. "Could we please make a quick stop at the farmers market?"

The middle-aged man nodded and merged into the parking lot.

"We have to make this quick," Caleb said as the van steered into a parking space. "Your *aenti* and *onkel* are expecting us. They know that our train arrived less than an hour ago and will worry if we don't get to their house soon."

"I'll be quick. I promise." Susie nodded, and the ties to her black winter bonnet bobbed up and down on her black wrap. "We should find a nice pie to bring for *Aenti* Sadie."

"That sounds *gut*." Caleb touched her nose and smiled. Oh how he adored his little girl. There was no greater love in his life.

Except for Barbara.

Pushing the thought from his mind, he took Susie's little hand in his and they climbed from the van. He glanced across the parking lot toward the highway, and his eyes fell on the Kauffman & Yoder Amish Furniture Store, owned by an old family friend, Eli Kauffman. Caleb's elder sister, Sadie, had married Robert, the oldest of the Kauffman sons, while the youngest Kauffman son, Timothy, had been Caleb's best school friend. He wondered how his old friend was doing these days. He would have to stop by and visit him before he and Susie returned to Ohio.

"*Dat*!" Susie yanked Caleb toward the entrance to the farmers market. "Let's go."

Caleb stifled a laugh. The little girl had her mother's impatience too. "I'm coming, *mei liewe*."

They stepped through the double doors and the holiday smells of freshly baked cookies and breads, spices, and pine assaulted Caleb's senses. The market bustled with customers, English and Amish, rushing to the many booths. Scanning the area, Caleb spotted booths for baked goods, jellies and jams, crafts and gifts, and paintings. A sea of shoppers pushed past Caleb and he dropped his hold of Susie's hand as he approached the baked goods counter.

"What kind of pie did you want to get, Susie?" Caleb asked. "Do you think a pumpkin pie or apple?" When his daughter didn't answer, he turned around and found a group of English customers pushing toward the counter.

"Susie?" he called. "Susie?" He glanced through the crowd, finding only unfamiliar faces. "Susan? Susan?" Caleb's heart raced as he pushed through the knot of holiday shoppers, searching for his only child. "Susan!"

❦

Naomi King straightened a king-size Lone Star patterned quilt and glanced at her best friend Lilly Lapp, who was glancing through the order book. "I can't believe Christmas is next week. Where has the year gone?"

Lilly shook her head. "I don't know. That's a very good question." An English customer approached and began asking Lilly questions about custom ordering a queen-size quilt as a gift.

Turning her back to the counter, Naomi hummed to herself while mentally listing all she had to do before Christmas. She still needed to shop for her parents and her eight siblings. And then there was the baking for the cookie exchange. And she had to—

"Excuse me," a little voice asked, interrupting her mental tirade.

Naomi spun to find a little girl leaning over the counter and pointing toward the king-size Lone Star quilt Naomi was draping over a wooden dowel. "May I help you?"

The girl adjusted the black bonnet on her head. "Did you make that?"

Naomi nodded. "*Ya*, I did."

"It's *schee*." The girl studied the quilt, her eyebrows knitting together in concentration. "My *mamm* made a quilt like this once, only she used blues and creams instead of maroons."

Naomi smiled. "I bet that was *schee*."

"Can I touch it?"

"Of course." Naomi held the quilt out, and the girl ran her hand over it.

The girl studied the quilt, her eyes trained on the intricate star pattern. "My *mamm* promised she would teach me how to quilt someday."

"I bet she will. I think I was about your age when my *mamm* started teaching me."

The girl looked up, and Naomi was struck by her deep green eyes. They reminded Naomi of the deep green the pasture turned every spring.

"My *mamm* is gone," the girl said, her expression serious.

"Gone?" Naomi set the dowel in the rack and leaned over the counter. "What do you mean?"

"She's in heaven with Jesus." The girl ran her fingers over the counter.

Naomi gasped, cupping a hand to her mouth. "I'm so sorry. You must miss her."

"I do. I was only—" she began.

"Susan!" A man rushed over, his expression full of fear. He placed his hands on the girl's shoulders and angled her to face him. He crouched down and met her at eye level. "I turned my head for a moment and you took off. Do you know how much you scared me? I thought I'd lost you. What were you thinking?"

"I'm sorry, *Dat*." The girl shook her head, tears filling her striking eyes. "I saw the quilt stand, and I wanted to come see the quilts."

The man sighed and closed his eyes for a split second. Standing, he took her hand in his. "Don't do that ever again." His voice pleaded with her. "Promise me?"

"*Ya*." A tear trickled down her rosy cheek, and she sniffed.

His expression became tender, and Naomi's heart swelled.

"Don't cry, Susie," he said, brushing her tears away with his fingertip. "It's okay, *mei liewe*. You're all right, and that's all that matters." He glanced toward the clock on the wall. "We need to get going. Your *aenti* is expecting us." He turned to Naomi. "I'm sorry for creating such a scene. My *dochder* took off and scared me so."

Naomi opened her mouth to speak, but her voice was stuck in her throat for a moment. Her eyes were lost in his, which were the same deep shade of emerald as the girl's.

"It was no bother," Naomi finally said. "We were having a nice discussion about quilts. I'm sorry she scared you."

"*Danki*." He glanced at his daughter. "We must be going." He turned back to Naomi. "*Frehlicher Grischtdaag*." He smiled, and his handsome face was kind. Yet, there was something sad in his gorgeous eyes. Naomi surmised it was the loss of his wife. Her heart ached for him.

Before she could respond to his Christmas greetings, the man and the girl were gone. He held the girl's hand as they turned the corner. The girl waved at Naomi, and Naomi waved back, her heart touched by the sweet gesture.

The customer who had been chatting with Lilly walked away from the stand.

"What happened?" Lilly asked, leaning over to Naomi.

"What?" Naomi asked, searching the crowd for the man and girl.

"What was all the commotion with the man and the girl?" Lilly closed the order book.

"The girl wandered off from her father, and he was worried about her." Naomi leaned against the counter. "She told me that her mother made quilts."

"Oh, that's sweet."

"*Ya*, it is." Naomi lifted a twin-size quilt from the bag below the counter and began to fold it. "But she also said her mother had died."

Lilly frowned and shook her head. "How *bedauerlich*."

"*Ya*, I know." Naomi glanced toward the door, wishing she could see the girl just one more time. "There was such sadness in her eyes. I saw it in her father's eyes too."

"I can imagine that the sadness was from losing her." Lilly

straightened the pens by the register. "I know how hard it was to lose my *mamm*, and I'm much older than she is."

Naomi touched Lilly's arm. "I know. There was just something ..." She let her voice trail off and pushed the thought away. She'd been burned more than once by misreading her own thoughts and feelings. It was silly to even consider she'd felt something for the man and the girl, but the feeling was strong, deep in her gut. She'd wanted to hug the girl and ask her how long her mother had been gone, to take away some of the pain in her eyes.

But that wasn't Naomi's business. She didn't even know the girl or her father. She'd never seen them before. She wondered which district they belonged to. Were they from Lancaster County or were they visiting for the holidays? Now she would never know. The moment was gone and so were the girl and her father.

"What is it?" Lilly asked, a grin splitting her pretty face. She jammed a hand on the hip of her purple frock. "You're scheming something, Naomi King."

"Don't be *gegisch*." Naomi draped the quilt over a dowel. "I was just thinking about that poor little girl without a mother. My heart goes out to her."

"Is that it? Or were you thinking about her father who misses his wife?"

Naomi frowned. "Please, Lilly. I don't know his name or even what district he's a member of. There's no such thing as love at first sight. Love is a feeling that grows over time. It can't just appear out of thin air."

Lilly's expression was pensive. "You're different than you were when you were seeing Timothy Kauffman."

Naomi shrugged. "No, I'm not different. I just matured. My *mamm* told me I was boy crazy and made a fool of myself the way I ran after Luke Troyer and then Timothy."

Lilly touched Naomi's shoulder. "That's not true. You were never a fool."

"*Ya*, I was." Naomi cleared her throat to prevent a lump from swelling in her throat as the humiliation rained down on her. She could still feel the sting of her mother's harsh words after she and Timothy broke up. "My *mamm* told me that I need to concentrate on my family and stop worrying about finding a husband. So, my focus now is my siblings. If I'm meant to find love, God will bring it into my life. But honestly, I think God wants me to help my *mamm* raise my eight siblings."

Lilly shook her head. "You don't honestly believe that, Naomi. God wants us to get married and have *kinner*."

Naomi busied herself with hanging the quilt onto the rack in order to avoid Lilly's probing stare. "*Ya*, I do believe it. I tried love twice and failed. That was the sign that I wasn't meant to find true love, if there even is a true love for me."

"Naomi." Lilly took Naomi's hand and gave her a gentle smile. "Listen to me. I didn't think there was a true love for me, but I was wrong."

Naomi raised an eyebrow in surprise. "You found love?"

Lilly's cheeks flushed a bright pink.

"Why haven't you told me?" Naomi asked. "I thought I was your best friend."

"You are." Lilly sighed and sat on a stool. "We were going to keep it a secret until we get published next year."

Naomi gasped. "You're getting married?"

Lilly smiled, and Naomi shrieked and hugged her.

"Is it Zach Fisher?" Naomi asked.

Lilly nodded. "I wanted to tell you, but we're trying to keep it a secret."

Naomi smiled. "That's *wunderbaar*. You deserve to be *froh*."

Lilly touched Naomi's arm. "You do too. God will lead you to the path He wants, and I believe He wants you to find true love. You've been hurt in the past, but that doesn't mean you're meant to be alone." She gave a gentle smile. "Just remember this verse from Corinthians: 'And our hope for you is firm, because we know that just as you share in our sufferings, so also you share in our comfort.'"

Naomi nodded in agreement, but she struggled to believe she was meant to be with someone.

"Excuse me," an English customer said, approaching the counter. "I would like to pick up a couple of quilts for my kids for Christmas. Do you have any queen-size quilts available that are Christmassy?"

"Yes, ma'am, we do," Lilly said, moving to the rack. "Let me show you what I have here."

As Lilly pulled out two quilts, Naomi glanced toward the market exit and wondered where the handsome widower and his daughter were headed when they left.

CHAPTER 2

The van bumped and rattled down the long rock driveway to his sister's large white farmhouse. The dairy farm had been passed down through the Schmucker family for four generations, and Caleb's parents had lived in the apartment at the back of the house until they passed away.

The white clapboard home still looked the same as he remembered from his childhood. The vast three stories sprawled across the front of the property, while one large white barn and three smaller barns sat behind it, housing their livestock and farming supplies. The white split-rail fence outlined the large pasture, and Sadie's gardens — her pride and joy that she replanted every spring — ran the length of the enormous house.

Happy childhood memories swirled through Caleb's mind. He'd spent many hours on the porch with his parents and extended family during the warm months. The back pasture was where he and his cousins would play baseball.

During his teenage years, the pasture became the site for impromptu volleyball courts during youth socials. And it was at one of those socials where he'd met Barbara, who'd been visiting her cousin for the summer. Caleb had taken one look at Barbara's beautiful smile, and he knew he'd met his future bride.

"*Dat?*" Susie's little voice brought him back to the present. "We're here, *ya?*"

Caleb leaned over and touched her chin. "*Ya,* we are." He glanced toward the porch and found his seven nieces and nephews filing out from the front door. "You go ahead and greet your cousins. I'll grab our bags and pay the driver."

"I can't wait to meet them!" Gripping the pumpkin pie in her hands, Susie trotted up the front steps to the circle of cousins.

After grabbing their two bags, Caleb paid the driver and then made his way up the front steps, where he was engulfed in hugs from his nieces and nephews.

"Caleb!" Sadie's voice rang through the crowd. "It's so *gut* to see you!" She pulled him into a tight hug. "How was your trip?"

"*Gut,*" he said.

"We were beginning to worry about you," Sadie said.

"We made a stop on the way," Caleb said, glancing at his daughter, who bit her bottom lip. "Susie wanted to bring you a pie."

"This is for you, *Aenti* Sadie." Susie handed her the pie. "We stopped at the farmers market for it."

"Oh, it smells *appeditlich.*" After hugging Susie, Sadie motioned for them to come into the house. "*Kumm!* Let's eat!"

Caleb sat between his nephews, Samuel and Raymond, at his sister's long kitchen table. Across from him, Susie was engrossed in an animated conversation with her cousins about school.

Robert cleared his throat and Caleb bowed his head in silent prayer. The aroma of baked chicken and freshly baked bread filled his senses and he smiled. Being surrounded by family warmed his soul, and he thanked God for the opportunity to spend Christmas with them.

When Robert's fork scraped the plate, Caleb glanced up at the gaggle of arms resembling an octopus reaching for the dishes and bowls of food in the center of the table. Voices rang out around him as the children discussed the upcoming Christmas plans.

"Caleb," Sadie said, raising her voice above the discussions swirling around them. "It's so *gut* to have you here with us. How does it feel to be home again?"

"*Gut*." Caleb glanced at his daughter, who was laughing while her cousin Janie shared a story. "Real *gut*." He loved seeing Susie so happy. He wished they had close relatives back home, but Barbara's cousins lived in a neighboring district and rarely visited.

"How are things in Middlefield?" Robert asked.

"Going well." Caleb grabbed the serving fork for the chicken.

"Is the carriage shop keeping you busy?" Robert asked while cutting up his chicken.

"*Ya*," Caleb said. "The buggy orders have been steady." He filled his plate with chicken and then grabbed a roll. "The Lord is blessing us with plenty of business. How is the dairy business?"

Robert shrugged. "The same. Every time we get ahead,

something happens to set us back, like the rising cost of diesel to run the milkers. There's always something holding us back."

Sadie beamed at her husband. "However, the Lord always provides."

Caleb asked Samuel about the youth gatherings, and soon their plates were clean and the serving dishes were empty.

While Sadie and the girls cleaned up the kitchen, Caleb joined Robert and the boys in the family room. The conversations spanned the hours as Caleb caught up with the latest community news. Susie rushed by, laughing and talking with her cousins as they stomped up the stairs to the bedrooms. Sadie brought in large hunks of pumpkin pie covered in whipped cream, and Caleb ate until his stomach was sore.

"We better get these *kinner* to bed," Sadie said when the clock struck eight. "Service is early in the morning tomorrow."

"*Ya.*" Caleb stood and stretched. "I'll tuck Susie in over in the apartment, *ya?*"

Sadie shook her head. "The girls want Susie to stay with them, but you're welcome to stay in the apartment if you'd like."

"That sounds *gut.*" Caleb carried Susie's bag up the steep stairs to the hallway lined with doors. He felt as if he'd been transported back in time since he'd climbed these stairs thousands of times during his childhood.

He found Susie giggling on a double bed with Janie and Linda. When she spotted Caleb in the doorway, they sat up.

"Girls!" Sadie bellowed, joining him in the doorway. "There's no need for all of this noise. You know that your *dat* likes some quiet in the evenings. You don't want him yelling, do you?"

Sadie's daughters silently shook their heads in response.

"*Gut*," Sadie continued. "Have you gotten your baths?"

They shook their heads no.

"It's time." Sadie stepped into the room and yanked nightgowns from the bureau.

The girls moaned their disappointment.

"Church comes early in the morning." Sadie pointed toward the hallway. "Go get your baths and then come to bed." She glanced at Caleb and smiled. "Let me go check on the boys. I'll be back."

Caleb turned to Susie. "Let's find your gown. You can take a bath too." He placed her bag on the bed and rummaged through it.

Susie sighed. "But I took a bath Thursday night."

He tried to suppress his smile. "*Ya*, but you were also cooped up on a smelly train overnight, and we have services tomorrow. Do you want the other *kinner* in the district to call you the stinky girl from Ohio?"

"No!" She laughed.

"Here." He pulled her bed clothes from the bag. "Now remember to keep your voice down. Your *onkel* doesn't like a lot of noise. We don't want to wear out our welcome on the first night. Go wash up."

Susie removed her prayer covering and unwound her long, light brown hair from its tight bun. She started for the door and then faced him, her pretty face pensive. "*Dat*, I'm sorry for scaring you at the market."

Caleb lowered himself on the bed and sighed. "I forgive you, *mei liewe*. I may be a bit overprotective, but it's my job to make sure you're safe." *Like I failed to do with your mother . . .*

He pushed the thought away. He needed to suppress that regret and concentrate on enjoying Christmas with his sister's family.

"I know." She bit her lower lip and then smiled. "Did you see that pretty lady at the quilt stand?"

"What pretty lady?" Sadie rounded the corner with her eyes wide with excitement.

Caleb swallowed a groan. While he loved his sister dearly, he'd learned a long time ago that she was a hopeless gossip, who enjoyed sharing the latest community news at her weekly quilting bees. Rumors of his courting Barbara spread like wildfire after Sadie caught Caleb and Barbara chatting on the porch late one night during the summer they met.

"At the farmers market, where we got the pie," Susie said, hugging her nightgown to her chest. "She was at a quilt stand, and she said that her *mamm* taught her how to make quilts when she was about my age."

"Quilt stand?" Sadie tilted her head in question. "That must have been Naomi King or maybe Lilly Lapp. They both work there. Naomi's *mamm* owns the stand. She's had it for years, and it does a good bit of business. I quilt for her sometimes."

"Really?" Susie's eyes were wide with excitement. "Would you teach me how to quilt, *Aenti* Sadie?"

"*Ya.*" Sadie touched Susie's nose. "Now you run along and get your bath. We must rise early in the morning."

"Okay." Susie trotted down the long hallway.

"She needs a *mamm*," Sadie said, shooting Caleb a stern look. "It's been two years."

Caleb frowned. He'd expected a lecture with Sadie's unsolicited advice, but he'd hoped she'd wait a day or two before starting in on him. "She has plenty of female role models in our community. She loves her teacher, and we have many friends at church."

"That's not the same as a *mamm*." Sadie's expression softened, and she stepped toward him. "She needs someone to be there when she has questions that only a woman can discuss."

Caleb pinched the bridge of his nose in hopes of stopping the tension headache brewing behind his eyes. "I know you mean well, but you can't tell me how to run my—"

"Naomi King wouldn't be a good match for you." Sadie talked over him while shaking her head. "She's a bit too eager for a husband. You know the type—always mingling with the men after service and trying to get them to go for rides with her."

"Sadie," Caleb said, attempting to interrupt her, but she continued her monologue as if she'd never heard him.

"Naomi ran after Luke Troyer, who married Sarah Rose, Robert's youngest sister, a couple of months ago," Sadie frowned. "Then she enticed Timothy Kauffman, but they broke up." She smiled. "I have just the *maedel* for you. There haven't been any rumors about her, and she's very sweet."

"Sadie," he repeated, standing.

Her grin widened with excitement. "Her name is Irene, and her *daed* owns a carriage shop. She'd be a *wunderbaar mamm* for Susie. You could move back here and go to work for her *daed* and—"

"Sadie!" His booming voice caused her to jump. "I'm sorry for startling you, but you're not listening to me. I'm not looking for a *mamm* for Susie just yet. Barbara was the love of my life, and I'm not ready to try to replace her."

"You won't ever replace her, Caleb." Sadie touched his arm. "You'll find a new *liewe*, who will help ease the pain and give Susie the guidance that only a *mamm* can give her. I know it's hard, but it's time to move on."

What do you know about loss? He swallowed the thought and glanced toward the door. "I think I'm going to go get ready for bed. Will you call me when the girls are ready to be tucked in?" He started for the door.

"*Ya*," Sadie said. "Caleb."

He faced her, hoping she wouldn't lecture him again. "*Ya?*"

"Please think about what I said." She stepped toward the door with a hopeful expression. "You and Susie are more than welcome to stay with us. You can move into the apartment, and Susie would love to go to school with her cousins. She needs her family, Caleb. Barbara was an only child, and her parents are gone. Who do you really have in Ohio?"

Caleb folded his arms in defiance. "We have family. Barbara had cousins, and our church district is *wunderbaar*. We're not alone."

"Think about it." She clasped her hands together. "I want you to meet Irene and consider my offer."

He nodded, knowing she wasn't going to let this issue die until he agreed. "Fine. I'll consider it."

"*Gut!*" She hugged him. "I'll call you when it's time to kiss Susie goodnight."

As Caleb descended the stairs, he hoped Sadie wouldn't spend his entire visit trying to play matchmaker. He wasn't ready for another relationship, and he believed Susie was receiving all the female guidance she needed. While Sadie had the best intentions, her meddling was misguided. He was a grown man and capable of making the best decisions for his child; Sadie needed to concentrate on her own family.

Caleb plucked his bag from the family room floor, then stepped through the doorway and into the apartment at the back of the house.

He moved through the small sitting room to the bedroom. As he placed the bag on the bed, he thought of the young woman at the farmers market. While he didn't know her name, he'd noticed her beautiful face and captivating brown eyes. She seemed to have made an impression on Susie. He wondered if he would run into her again during his visit.

Deep in his heart, he hoped he would.

CHAPTER 3

Naomi sat with the other young unmarried women while she sang along with the familiar German hymns in the *Ausbund*. Keeping with tradition, the three-hour service was held in the home of one of the church district families on every other Sunday. With the living room and bedroom moveable walls removed, the downstairs of Eli and Elizabeth Kauffman's home was spacious. Backless benches were lined up for the district members, and later they would be converted to tables for lunch.

The congregation was seated by age and gender, and the service area was plain. There was no altar, no cross, no flowers, nor instruments. They sang the hymns slowly, and a male song leader chosen at the beginning of the service would begin the first syllable of each line.

While the ministers met in another room for thirty minutes to choose who would preach that day, the congregation continued to sing. They returned during the last verse of the second hymn, which was always *"Lob Lied,"* and when the ministers hung their hats on the pegs on the wall, it symbolized that the service was about to begin.

The minister began the first sermon, and Naomi clasped

her hands. Her eyes scanned the congregation, and she tried to concentrate on the minister's words. However, her thoughts kept fluttering to the scene at the farmers market yesterday. She could still visualize the little girl's sweet face when she shared that her mother had died. The fear mixed with relief on the father's face was still fresh in Naomi's mind—along with his expressive eyes.

She was still thinking of him when her stare moved to the married men sitting across the room. She spotted Robert Kauffman, and her gaze stopped when her eyes focused on the man next to him. She blinked, but the figure didn't transform. The man from the market was sitting next to Robert Kauffman.

How can this be?

The man's eyes met hers, and he looked as surprised as she felt. A smile turned up the corners of his mouth, and Naomi felt her cheeks burn with embarrassment.

Why was this stranger causing her to blush? She didn't even know him! She quickly looked away in order to break the trance.

The first sermon ended, and Naomi knelt in silent prayer along with the rest of the congregation. During her prayers, she pushed thoughts of the stranger from her mind and thanked God for the blessings in her life. She also asked for health and happiness for her family during the upcoming holidays.

After the prayers, the deacon read from the Scriptures and then the hour-long main sermon began. Naomi tried in vain to keep her eyes off the stranger during the sermon, but her glance kept moving back to him. He occasionally met her gaze with a pleasant smile, and each time, her heart fluttered and cheeks flushed. She stared at her lap and willed herself to concentrate on the sermon, which was always spoken in High German, keeping with Amish tradition.

She swallowed a sigh of relief when the kneeling prayer was over. The congregation then stood for the benediction, and the closing hymn was sung.

When the service was over, Naomi moved toward the kitchen with the rest of the women to help serve the noon meal. The men converted the benches into tables and then sat and chatted while awaiting their food. As she headed for the kitchen, Naomi averted her eyes from the group of men talking in the corner since she'd spotted the mysterious widower speaking to Timothy Kauffman.

"The service was beautiful, *ya*?" Kathryn Beiler asked Naomi as she moved a tray of pies and cakes over to the counter covered in the desserts.

"*Ya*, it was," Naomi agreed, filling a pitcher of water.

"Are you ready for Christmas?" Kathryn asked.

Naomi laughed. "No. I still need some things to finish my gifts. How about you?"

Kathryn shook her head. "No, I'm not ready either. Perhaps we should go shopping to—"

"Hi!" A little voice screeched. "Hi!"

Naomi glanced over just as Susie came trotting toward her with Robert and Sadie Kauffman's two youngest daughters trailing close behind. "Susie?"

"I remember you from the farmers market!" The little girl beamed. "So this is your church district?"

"*Ya*, it is." Naomi gestured toward Janie and Linda. "I see you know Janie and Linda Kauffman."

Susie took their hands in hers. "They're my cousins. I just met them for the first time yesterday, and we're already best friends."

Naomi plastered a smile on her lips as she inwardly gasped—Susie and her father were related to the Kauffmans! She hoped that meeting Susie wouldn't become awkward. While the Kauffmans had been gracious after her breakups with Luke and Timothy, she still felt uncomfortable. She could only imagine the rumors that were still flying about her and how forward she was with the boys.

"You know Susie?" Kathryn asked, sidling up to Naomi.

"We met at the farmers market yesterday," Naomi said.

Susie beamed. "She makes *schee* quilts like my *mamm* did."

"*Ya*," Kathryn said, smiling. "She does." She turned to Naomi. "Susie and her *dat* are visiting from Ohio for the holidays. Her *dat* is Sadie's *bruder*."

"Oh," Naomi said with a nod while suppressing an inward groan. "That's so nice."

"What's your name?" Susie asked.

"I'm Naomi," she said, shaking the girl's hand. "It's nice to meet you."

"You too," Susie said.

A chorus of voices sounded as a group of women entered the kitchen laughing, including Beth Anne Bontrager, one of Timothy's sisters, and Miriam Lapp, Timothy's fiancée.

Beth Anne's eyes widened as she approached. "Susie!" She hugged the little girl. "I saw your *dat*, and I was looking for you. How are you?"

"*Gut*." Susie gave her a shy smile.

Beth Anne smiled. "You don't know me, do you?"

Susie bit her bottom lip and shook her head. "I'm sorry, but I haven't met you yet."

"She's *Aenti* Beth Anne," Janie said.

"I'm your *Onkel* Robert's sister," Beth Anne said. "And this is Miriam. She's *Onkel* Timothy's fiancée."

Naomi slowly backed up toward the counter. She wanted to sneak away and hide somewhere far away from this uncomfortable moment. Pushing thoughts of Susie and her father out of her mind, she crossed the kitchen and found her mother. She planned to help serve lunch and forget her idea of getting to know Susie.

❦

"Caleb!" A voice bellowed. "Caleb Schmucker!"

Caleb turned just as Timothy Kauffman smacked his back. "Timothy!"

"How are you?" Timothy gave his hand a stiff shake. "It's been what—ten years?"

"It feels that long. I'm *gut*." Caleb examined his face and found it clean shaven. "You're not married yet?"

Timothy smirked. "I'm working on it."

"What are you waiting for?" Caleb asked. "You're thirty now. We're getting old."

Timothy laughed. "*Ya*, we are, but I'm getting there. I think next wedding season I'll be taking my vow with my *liewe*. How's Susie? I believe I saw her running off with Robert's girls."

"She is doing well," Caleb said. He patted Timothy's shoulder. "It's so *gut* to see you. I've missed my family here."

Timothy shrugged. "So move back. You can build buggies here just like you do in Middlefield."

Caleb scanned the room, spotting a host of familiar faces. "It's tempting."

Timothy guided Caleb to a table where they sat with Timothy's brothers and a few other men Caleb recognized. "I think a new start would be *wunderbaar* for you and Susie."

"How are you, Caleb?" Daniel Kauffman asked, leaning over and shaking Caleb's hand.

"It's so *gut* to see you," Eli Kauffman interjected. "I was so sorry to hear about Barbara."

"*Danki*," Caleb said with a nod.

"How are things in Ohio?" Eli asked.

He updated the men on his life, and out of the corner of his eye, he spotted the woman from the farmers market. She approached the table with a tray of potato salad, and he tried to make eye contact.

"*Danki*, Naomi," Daniel said as she filled his plate with potato salad.

Naomi. Her name is Naomi.

Caleb let the name roll through his mind while he tried to remember what Sadie had told him about her. According to Sadie, the woman was too eager for a husband and she had run after Luke Troyer and Timothy. However, she looked very sweet and humble with her pretty face and deep brown eyes. He couldn't imagine her running after any man.

While the conversation at his table continued among the men, Caleb tried again to make eye contact with her. However, she quickly served each of them and then moved on to the adjacent table. He wondered if she'd even seen him. He'd noticed her during the service, and she'd met his gaze. Why was she avoiding it now?

Naomi headed back to the kitchen, and Caleb felt the unfaltering urge to follow her. He set his fork on the table and stood.

"Caleb?" Timothy asked, looking confused.

Caleb nodded toward the kitchen. "I'm going to go check on Susie. I'll be right back." He headed toward the kitchen but was waylaid by David Beiler, who stepped in front of him, blocking the doorway.

"How are you, Caleb?" David shook his hand. "It's so good to see you."

"It's nice to see you too. I spoke to Kathryn earlier." Caleb glanced past him, spotting Naomi chatting with an older woman while filling another pan with potato salad.

"Caleb!" Sadie said, appearing with a tray of rolls. "I've been looking for you. I have someone I want you to meet."

Caleb glanced back toward the kitchen doorway just as Naomi stepped through it. She met his stare and then quickly turned away. Before he could step toward her, Sadie grabbed his arm and yanked him to the other side of the room, causing him to stumble along behind her.

"Sadie, I was going to—" he began.

"Caleb," she said, bringing him to a jolting stop in front of an attractive young blonde, who smiled. "This is Irene Wagler. Irene's *daed* owns Wagler's Buggies in Intercourse."

"*Wie geht's?*" Irene held out her hand.

Caleb gave her hand a quick shake. "It's nice to meet you."

Irene glanced toward the kitchen. "I better get back in and finish serving the drinks."

"Don't be silly," Sadie said, waving off the comment. "You two get acquainted, and I'll bring out the drinks." She winked at Irene, and Caleb wondered if she'd meant to be discreet. However, he was certain his older sister had never been subtle a day in her life.

"Sadie tells me you're visiting for the holidays," Irene said as she leaned against the wall behind her.

"*Ya.*" Caleb fingered his beard and glanced across the room where Naomi was scooping potato salad onto a man's plate.

"You should come by and see my *daed's* shop. It's very nice."

"Maybe I will," he said.

Susie raced over, narrowly missing running into a man who was headed in the opposite direction. "*Dat! Dat!*"

"Calm down," he told her, leaning over to take her hand in his. "You almost crashed into that man."

"*Dat!*" Her eyes were wide with excitement. "*Aenti* Sadie told me that I'm going to a cookie exchange tomorrow! Isn't that *wunderbaar?*" She squeezed his hands. "I love it here."

He laughed. "That sounds *wunderbaar gut.* I'm so glad you're having fun." He nodded toward Irene. "This is my new friend, Irene. Can you say hello to her?"

"Hi. I'm Susan Schmucker, but my friends call me Susie."

"Hi, Susie. I'm Irene, and I'll be at the cookie exchange tomorrow too." Although Irene smiled down at his daughter, Caleb couldn't help but notice that the smile didn't reach her eyes.

"I'm going to go back in the kitchen and help with the dishes," Susie said. "Bye!"

Caleb grinned after her. Oh how that little girl warmed his heart.

"So, tell me about Middlefield," Irene said.

He shrugged. "What do you want to know?"

Irene smiled, and this one was real. "Everything."

CHAPTER 4

"How are you really?" Timothy asked. "You said things are *gut* at work, but how are you really coping?"

Caleb shivered while sitting on the porch at Eli Kauffman's house later that evening. Most everyone had left, except for a few families, the bulk of them related to the Kauffmans. He was disappointed that he hadn't managed to speak with Naomi before she exited with her family. However, he'd shared a brief gaze with her from across the crowded room. She'd given him a shy smile, and he noticed she had an adorable dimple on her right cheek. He hated how cliché the smile across the crowded room felt, and he hoped he'd meet her personally soon.

"Caleb?" Timothy asked. "Did you hear me? I asked how you truly are. You can be honest with me."

Caleb buried his frigid hands in the pockets of his coat. "I'm living, day to day. Susie keeps me going."

Timothy frowned. "How's Susie coping?"

Caleb shrugged. "She seems okay to me. She loves school, and her teacher is *wunderbaar.*" He shook his head. "Sadie told me last night that Susie needs a *mamm*, but it's not that simple. I can't just order one from a catalog."

Timothy gave a bark of laughter. "Mail order *mamm*, eh?"

"Right." Caleb chuckled.

"There's no one special waiting for you back in Ohio?"

"No." Caleb shook his head. "One of Barbara's cousins tried to set me up with a couple of her friends, but we really didn't have anything in common. Her cousin finally gave up on me."

Timothy turned to him, looking intrigued. "Don't you want to find a *mamm* for Susie? I don't mean to sound like your *schweschder*, but why would you want to raise Susie all by yourself?"

"It's not that I choose to be alone, but it sort of feels like I'm supposed to be alone." Caleb paused, gathering his thoughts. He'd never opened up about this subject before and it made him uncomfortable. However, he trusted Timothy and he wanted to get the emotions out in the open. "I feel like I don't deserve to be *froh* after what happened to Barbara. I feel like it's my fault."

Timothy frowned. "It's not your fault, Caleb. It was an accident."

"I know," Caleb said with a sigh. "But it's not fair that I'm still here, and she's not. I feel like I should be punished or suffer somehow." He thought about the nights spent alone in bed, thinking of her and all they lost. "I feel like I'm stuck in this lonely cloud sometimes just floating around all by myself."

"Maybe you and Susie need a new beginning." Timothy brightened. "You can come back here and start over. That would cheer you up a bit and help you move on."

"It's not that easy. I also feel guilty about moving on with my life. How is it fair that I can move on, but Barbara can't?"

Timothy was silent for a moment. "What's keeping you in Ohio? What do you have there?"

"Susie has a few of Barbara's cousins that we see occasionally," Caleb said. "That seems to be the right reason to stay. But to be perfectly honest, I'm not sure why we are stuck in the same old routine. I guess it's easy because I don't have to think about it. I just continue through the daily grind. The reminders of Barbara all over the house are painful, but I try to let go of my emotions and just remain distant. It's the only way I know to cope with it all for Susie's sake."

"So you're the shell of the man you once were?" Timothy shook his head. "That's sad."

Caleb paused, touching his beard while considering Timothy's words. He knew his friend was right, but he didn't want to talk about it anymore. He needed to change the subject. "I'd rather hear about your life, Timothy. When do I get to meet your future *fraa*?"

Timothy jammed a thumb toward the door. "Miriam is here. She was talking with my sisters earlier."

"How'd you meet her?"

Timothy shook his head. "It's a long story. We met at a singing."

"A singing?" Caleb sat up straight on the bench. "Your district has singings for folks our age? I definitely need to move back home."

"Ha, ha," Timothy muttered, his voice seeping sarcasm. "That's not what I meant. We met when we were younger, and then we parted ways. Miriam moved to Indiana for a few years and then came back last year. We worked things out, and now we're finally on the right path. I guess God needed us to grow up a bit before we were ready to get married."

"That may be so." *Is that why God took Barbara from me? Is there a lesson I need to learn before I find happiness again?* Caleb stared out at the small snowflakes beginning to fall from the sky while the thoughts floated through his mind. "We may have a white Christmas," he finally said.

"*Ya*," Timothy said. "It's supposed to snow a few times before Christmas Eve."

Caleb wanted to ask Timothy about Naomi. However, he didn't want to make it sound like he was interested in her. He didn't even know her, but he found her so intriguing. There was something about her, something subtle that he couldn't put into words. She was nothing like the women back in Ohio that Barbara's cousin had tried to push him to get to know.

"You should come by the furniture store," Timothy said, rubbing his hands together. "We rebuilt it after the fire, and it looks a bit different. It's a little bigger. We've been really busy this year. My *daed* hired a few more carpenters."

"I'm glad business is *gut*. I'd heard about the fire," Caleb said. "I'm sorry about Peter."

"*Ya*, that was a tragedy." Timothy frowned. "Much like what happened ..." His words trailed off, but Caleb knew he was speaking of Barbara.

Caleb didn't want to talk about the accident now and run the risk of getting emotional. "On the way in yesterday, Susie and I stopped at the farmers market, and she spoke to a woman at a quilt stand." He gestured toward the door. "The woman was here today. Her name is Naomi, and Susie has really taken to her. Do you know her?"

Timothy smiled. "*Ya*, you could say I know her."

Curious, Caleb raised an eyebrow. For some reason, he'd hoped the rumors Sadie had shared weren't true.

"I feel bad because I sort of broke her heart." Timothy shook his head. "You won't be proud of me, *bruder*."

"I'm certain it's nothing that you should be ashamed of, Timothy," Caleb said, hoping he wasn't going to regret asking about her.

"I guess you could say I led her on." Timothy stared off toward the falling snow. "We courted for a while, and I guess I sort of used her to get my mind off Miriam when Miriam came back into town. I feel terrible about it. I was going to keep my word and stay with Naomi, but she set me free, saying she knew I loved Miriam and not her. Naomi seems so sad now. I feel bad about it, but I couldn't live a lie either. If I had married Naomi, we would've wound up resenting each other."

Caleb nodded, letting the words sink in. As usual, Sadie had it wrong. From what Timothy had described, Naomi wasn't a desperate woman; she'd simply had her heart broken.

"But Naomi is a real nice *maedel*. We're still friends." Timothy hugged his coat to his chest. "It's cold, *ya*?"

"It is December," Caleb said. "What did you expect—a heat wave?"

Timothy chuckled. "I'm glad to see you're still a wise guy."

The door opened and banged shut, and Robert stepped out. "It's cold out here. How can you sit out here and talk?"

"We can hear our thoughts out here, unlike in there," Timothy said with a smile.

Robert chuckled. "*Ya*, the women and *kinner* are loud."

He looked toward the road. "I guess we better get going. The animals will be hungry." He stepped back toward the door. "I'll gather everyone up."

Timothy stood. "We'll get the buggies hitched."

Caleb followed him to the barn. "It was *gut* visiting with you."

"You should come by the shop and see me this week," Timothy said as he opened the barn door.

"*Ya*, I will." Caleb led Robert's horse from the stall.

"You really should think about moving back here," Timothy repeated, leading his horse out of the barn. "I know you could get a job building buggies here, or you could even start your own business. I'm certain you could get a loan and find some land." Timothy snapped his fingers. "In fact, there's some land with a big shop for sale by the furniture store. If you'd like, I could contact the owner and tell him—"

"Whoa!" Caleb held his hand up to silence his friend. "Slow down, Timothy. I just arrived yesterday, and I didn't come with the intention of moving back."

Timothy grinned. "I know you didn't come with that intention, but you could leave with it."

"Timothy!" a woman's voice called. "Are we leaving? It's getting late."

"Caleb," Timothy said with a sweeping gesture as the brunette approached. "This is Miriam Lapp. Miriam, this is Caleb Schmucker, my best friend from boyhood. He's visiting from Ohio for Christmas."

Caleb shook her hand. "It's nice to meet you."

"You too," she said with a smile. "I met your daughter, Susie. She's a cutie."

"*Danki*." Caleb hitched Robert's horse to the buggy while Timothy hitched his. "I guess I'll see you again," he said, climbing into the buggy seat.

"*Ya*," Timothy said. "I expect to see you."

"You will." Caleb drove the buggy up to the porch, and Robert, Sadie, and the children piled in. As he steered onto the main road and headed toward their house, the children chattered about the upcoming school Christmas program.

He smiled as they talked, their voices filled with excitement, and he watched the snowflakes pelt the windshield. His thoughts turned to Naomi and Timothy's story of how he broke her heart. He longed to talk to Naomi, to get to know her. But why? Why should he think of this woman when he was only going to be in town a short while?

Unless he took Timothy's advice and stayed ...

He pushed the thoughts away as the horse clip-clopped down the road. He would only concentrate on spending time with his family. That was all that mattered. His family would get him through the second anniversary of Barbara's death. He needed them now.

CHAPTER 5

"Why do I have to go?" Naomi asked as she placed more cookies into the five-gallon bucket at her feet. "You can take my sisters and then bring them back when it's over."

Lilly tapped her finger on the counter with impatience. "Naomi, we discussed this. You're expected to be at this cookie exchange."

"No, I'm not." Naomi continued to drop cookies into the bucket. "I don't belong there. Sarah Rose and Miriam will both be there for sure. It's going to be at the Kauffmans' bakery, so it's a Kauffman event."

"So?" Lilly threw up her hands. "You're a friend of the Kauffman family."

"But you were invited, not me," Naomi said, dropping the last of the sugar cookies into the bucket, filling it to the brim. "You're Miriam's sister. I'm just an ex-fiancée. You can't get much more awkward than that."

Lilly swiped an extra cookie from the counter. "You're the only one who thinks it's awkward. My sister happens to like you, and all the Kauffman sisters talk to you every time they see you. The only awkwardness is what you perceive in your head." She bit the cookie and moaned. "These cookies are delicious. You really outdid yourself."

"*Danki*," Naomi muttered.

"You really need to get over this idea that the Kauffmans don't like you. It's simply not true," Lilly said, lowering herself into a kitchen chair. "My sister is going to be a Kauffman, so that makes me a Kauffman by default. You're my best friend, so you're going to have to hang out with me and the Kauffmans."

"You could never understand how I feel," Naomi's voice quavered as she swept the crumbs from the counter into the palm of her hand. "Every time I see them, I think of how I made a fool of myself. It's hard to relive it over and over again."

"You didn't make a fool of yourself," Lilly said. "You were just immature."

Naomi nodded. "I know. I pursued Luke in a very unladylike way by running after him and bringing him lunch all the time. I never should've chased after him."

Lilly gave a sad smile. "You didn't realize you were doing that. You thought you were in love with Luke, but it was really a crush. On the other hand, you didn't pursue Timothy. He courted *you*." She pointed to Naomi for emphasis. "He proposed to you and then changed his mind, breaking your heart in the process."

"That's true," Naomi began, "but I think I went about it all the wrong way with both of them. I was so eager, and I was trying to make my future happen instead of waiting for God's plan." She sniffed.

"*Ach.*" Lilly stood and touched Naomi's shoulder. "I didn't mean to upset you."

"It's okay." Naomi wiped away her threatening tears and shook her head.

"The Kauffmans are members of your church district," Lilly said softly. "You can't avoid them unless you stop going to church."

Naomi leaned against the counter and swiped a cookie from the bucket. "Sometimes I dream of marrying someone from another district, so I don't have to see them every other Sunday. Is that *gegisch*?"

Lilly snorted. "*Ya*, it's *gegisch*. How can you marry someone from another district if you don't visit other districts? Do you think an eligible bachelor will fall from heaven and transport you into another church district?"

Naomi glowered.

"I'm sorry." Lilly smiled. "Naomi, I'm just trying to tell you that you have every right to go to this cookie exchange. The Kauffmans like you, and they want you there. How will it look if I show up with your sisters and you're absent?"

"Tell them I'm ill." Naomi bit into the cookie. "These cookies aren't half bad."

"It would be a lie if I told them you're ill, and lying is a sin. I'm not going to knowingly sin this close to Christmas." Lilly crossed the kitchen to the doorway heading into the family room. "Lizzie Anne! Levina! Sylvia!" She bellowed each of Naomi's sisters' names.

The girls raced into the kitchen, chattering all at once.

"Lilly!" Lizzie Anne, who was fifteen, hugged her. "*Wie geht's?*"

"Is it time to go yet?" Sylvia, who was eight, whined. "I want cookies!"

53

"We're going to be late!" Levina, who was ten, pulled on her wrap and bonnet and headed out the door, announcing she was ready to go.

Lilly shot Naomi a smile. "Are you ready?"

"No," Naomi muttered. She snatched her wrap from the peg by the door and moved to the doorway, where she spotted her mother sitting in her favorite chair quilting. "We're leaving," she told her mother.

"Have fun," her mother said with a smile.

"*Ya.*" Naomi crossed the kitchen and grabbed the bucket of cookies. She instructed Lizzie Anne and Sylvia to carry the two covered dishes to the buggy. "Elam should have the buggy waiting for us. *Daed* told him to hook it up earlier."

"Your *mamm's* not coming?" Lilly asked as she tied her bonnet under her chin.

"No," Naomi said, heading for the door. "She has some last-minute quilts to finish. They're Christmas orders that an English customer is going to pick up later in the week. We're going to have a quilting bee at Sadie's on Wednesday to finish them up." She sighed as her sisters rushed out the door. "Let's get this over and done with."

"Naomi," Lilly began with a condescending smile. "It's Christmas. Get in the Christmas spirit."

Naomi rolled her eyes. "I can't wait until this Christmas season is over and we can get back to our normal lives."

Lilly's smile faded. "You don't mean that."

Frowning, Naomi placed the bucket on the counter. "No, I don't mean it, really. The *kinner* are excited." Her eyes filled with tears, and she suddenly felt like a heel. "I'm very blessed. I have a *wunderbaar* family and *freinden* like you.

54

But sometimes I feel selfish and wish I had someone special to share the holidays with." Clearing her throat, she lifted the bucket. "But that's a selfish and *gegisch* thing to say. Let's go."

"No, it's okay." Lilly touched Naomi's arm. "You'll find your special someone."

"Naomi!" Sylvia's voice shrieked. "It's cold out here!"

Shaking her head, Naomi headed for the door. She hoped the cookie exchange would be quick and painless.

✻

With her sisters laughing and chattering in the back, Naomi guided the horse as the buggy bounced along the road leading to the Kauffman Amish Bakery. The terrain was hilly, and the roads were winding and rural. Soon she spotted the Kauffman farm with a cluster of large houses set back off the road and surrounded by four barns, along with a large pasture dotted with snow.

The property was owned by Elizabeth and Eli Kauffman, Timothy's parents, and included their house, Timothy's house, and Sarah and Luke Troyer's house. The bakery was the fourth house, the one closest to the road. Timothy and his five siblings had grown up in the biggest house, where his parents still lived.

Naomi steered into the parking lot and brought it to a stop by a row of buggies. A tall sign with *Kauffman Amish Bakery* in old-fashioned letters hung above the door of the large, white clapboard farmhouse with the sweeping wrap-around porch.

Out behind the building was a fenced-in play area, and beyond that was an enclosed field. The three other large farmhouses and four barns were set back beyond the pasture. The dirt road leading to the other homes was roped off with a sign declaring: *Private Property — No Trespassing.* A large paved parking lot sat adjacent to the bakery.

"Cookies!" Sylvia yelled, trotting toward the steps.

"Yay!" Levina chimed in.

"Wait!" Lizzie Anne called. "You can carry something." She pulled the covered dishes from the back of the buggy. "Here. Take these."

The girls took the serving platters and hurried toward the bakery.

"Slow down!" Lizzie Anne called. Shaking her head, she hefted the bucket up from the buggy floor.

"*Danki,*" Naomi said while she and Lilly unhitched the horse. "You take the empty buckets, and I'll bring the cookies."

Lizzie Anne started toward the door, carrying the empty buckets that they would fill with cookies. "I'm going to see if Lindsay is here."

While Lilly led the horse to the pasture to join the other horses, Naomi grabbed the bucket of cookies and started toward the stairs. A sign on the door said: *Bakery Closed at 4 p.m. for Private Party.*

Lilly fell in step beside her. "Smile, Naomi," she said as they approached the door. "It's Christmas."

Plastering a smile on her face, Naomi yanked the door open and stepped into the bakery. The room was rearranged with a long line of tables placed in the center of the room with piles of cookies lined up from one end to the other. The counter was filled with a variety of covered dishes, which

Naomi assumed were desserts other than cookies. Women and girls of all ages were gathered around the table chatting. Naomi inhaled the delicious scents of cookies, cakes, breads, and casseroles.

"Naomi!" Susie yelled as she ran over and reached for the bucket. "Can I help you?"

Naomi couldn't stop the smile forming on her lips. "Hello, Susie." She handed the little girl the bucket. "Are you certain you can lift this? It's sort of heavy."

"I got it." Susie huffed and puffed, but she couldn't lift it.

Grinning, Naomi grabbed the handle. "Let me help you."

"That's a good idea. We'll work together." Susie put her little hand on the handle next to Naomi's, and they lifted together. Walking slowly, they moved to the table.

"On three, we'll lift the bucket onto the table," Naomi said. "One, two, three!"

They hefted the bucket onto an empty spot on the table and began to carefully remove the cookies.

"Teamwork," Susie said with a smile.

Elizabeth Kauffman stepped to the center of the room and clapped her hands. "Hello everyone!" she said. "I'm so glad you all could come to our cookie exchange. I'm sure you all remember the rules. We'll file around the table and fill our buckets until all of the cookies are gone." She motioned toward the counter behind her. "And then we'll enjoy our delicious desserts. *Frehlicher Grischtdaag!*"

Chattering and laughing, the women and girls lined up around the table.

Susie looked up at Naomi. "Can I help you get cookies?"

Naomi's heart warmed. "I would love it," she said.

Susie beamed and held up the bucket. "I'll get us the best cookies."

Touching Susie's shoulder, Naomi smiled. "That sounds *wunderbaar gut.*"

As they moved around the table grabbing cookies, Naomi wondered why Susie had latched onto her when there were a host of other women and Susie's cousins in the room. And would Susie's father approve if he saw Susie with her? Her thoughts turned to Susie's father, and she wondered what he was doing while they filled buckets with cookies.

❧

"This is nice," Caleb said. He glanced around the showroom of the Kauffman & Yoder Amish Furniture Store and marveled at the dining room sets, bedroom suites, entertainment centers, hutches, end tables, desks, and coffee tables. All were examples of the finely crafted pieces that Timothy and the other carpenters created.

Timothy's father, Eli, had built the original store with his best friend, Elmer Yoder, before Timothy was born.

"*Danki.*" Timothy looped an arm around Caleb's shoulder. "Let's go in the shop and you can see everyone."

Timothy led Caleb behind the counter and through the doorway to the center of the work area. Caleb scanned the sea of carpenters and waved at Timothy's brother, Daniel. The large, open warehouse was divided into nearly a dozen work areas separated by workbenches cluttered with an array of tools.

The sweet scent of wood and stain filled his nostrils. The men working around him were building beautifully designed pieces that would be favorites among Lancaster County tourists and residents alike. Hammers banged and saw blades whirled beneath the hum of diesel-powered air compressors.

Eli approached and shook Caleb's hand. *"Wie geht's?"*

"I'm doing well," Caleb said. "This is a *wunderbaar* shop you have. It's bigger, and the furniture is still *schee.*"

"Danki." Eli folded his arms and glanced around. "We're pleased with it. Business has been very *gut* this year. The Lord is *gut* to us."

Daniel approached with another man at his side. "Caleb! This is Luke Troyer, my sister Sarah's husband. Luke, this is a dear old friend, Caleb Schmucker. He abandoned us and moved to Ohio several years ago."

Caleb chuckled as he shook Luke's hand. "It's nice to meet you, and I didn't abandon anyone."

Luke laughed. "Nice to meet you too."

"Caleb builds buggies," Timothy said. "He's known in Middlefield as one of the best."

Caleb waved off the comment. "You're exaggerating."

"We could use your talent around here," Timothy said.

"You should have your own shop." Daniel patted Caleb's shoulder. "You need to move back here."

"That's funny," Caleb nodded. "I keep hearing that."

"I'm serious," Daniel continued. "Did you see that shop just down the road?" He pointed in the direction of the showroom. "It's not far from here. An Englisher owns it." He glanced at Eli. "What's his name?"

"Parker," Eli said, rubbing his beard. "Riley Parker."

Daniel snapped his fingers. "Right! He's been trying to sell it for quite a while. I bet you could get a great deal on it."

"That's a great idea," Luke chimed in. "We could help you fix the place up."

"*Ya*, we could," Timothy said with a grin.

"Hold on a minute!" Caleb held his hands up. "Slow down. I have a life in Ohio."

Timothy raised his eyebrows in question, and Caleb glanced away.

"Let's introduce you to the rest of the carpenters," Eli said. "Elmer would enjoy seeing you. It's been a long time."

After meeting all of the carpenters, Caleb sat in the break room with Timothy and Daniel. "Your *dat* has done well for himself."

Timothy passed a bottle of water across the table to Caleb. "*Ya*, he has. It's hard work, but it's paid off."

"Is Susie at the cookie party today?" Daniel asked while opening a bottle of water.

Caleb took a sip and nodded. "She was excited about it this morning. She loves being with her cousins."

Timothy raised his eyebrows.

Caleb shook his head. "Timothy, please don't start nagging me about moving here."

Timothy feigned insult. "I didn't say a word."

"Don't you think it would be good for Susie to be around her cousins and her family?" Daniel asked.

Caleb nodded. "I know it would be. I'm just not certain it will be good for me." He tore at the label on the bottle. "I'm not certain I'm ready to leave the memories."

"*Ach*," Timothy said. "Look at the time. The cookie

exchange will be over soon." He stood. "I told Miriam I'd pick her up." He glanced at his brother. "Are you going to get Rebecca and the girls?"

Daniel nodded. "I am."

"Do you want me to get them?" Timothy offered.

"Will you have room for everyone?" Daniel asked. "Rebecca has Lindsay and Daniel Jr."

Timothy shrugged. "I think we'll have plenty of room."

"That would be fine," Daniel said. "I can finish this project I started. *Danki*."

Caleb stood and shook Daniel's hand. "It was *gut* seeing you again."

"*Ya*," Daniel said. "Think about what I said about the property nearby. You'd have plenty of business here. I think a new start would be *gut* for your soul."

"I'll consider it," Caleb said.

He followed Timothy through the shop, where he said good-bye to the carpenters. Daniel's words were still fresh in his mind as he climbed into Timothy's buggy. Would moving be good for his soul? Would it be good for Susie, or would uprooting her from all she'd ever known cause her more emotional pain after losing her mother only two years ago? He thought back to the conversation he'd had with Timothy after the church service. While Caleb felt guilty about moving on, he was beginning to wonder if it was time to take the plunge and do it. Perhaps he should consider breaking free of the holding pattern he'd been stuck in since he'd lost Barbara. The questions rolled through his mind as they headed toward the bakery.

Susie sat across from Naomi at a small table and bit into another cookie. "I love chocolate chip cookies. They're my favorite. What's your favorite, Naomi?"

Naomi glanced beside her at Lilly, who grinned in response. "I think peanut butter is my favorite," Naomi said.

"Oh," Susie said. "I love peanut butter too. I guess I have two favorites." She turned to Janie beside her. "You like peanut butter, right?"

Janie nodded. "*Ya*, I love peanut butter. My *mamm* makes the best peanut butter cookies."

Susie glanced back at Naomi. "I like to bake. Do you like to bake?"

Naomi nodded. "I do."

"Do you bake a lot?" Susie asked between bites of cookie.

"*Ya*, I do. I have a big family, and I do a good bit of cooking." Naomi sipped her cup of water.

"How many brothers and sisters do you have?" Susie asked.

"I have five brothers and three sisters," Naomi said.

Susie's eyes widened. "Oh my. That is a big family. You're so lucky. I'm an only child." She frowned. "My *mamm* was going to have another *boppli* when she died."

Naomi dropped her cookie, and Lilly gasped.

Susie nodded. "*Ya*, my *dat* was so sad when my *mamm* died. I was sad too. I cried for my *mamm* and also for the *boppli*."

Naomi was stunned into silence for a moment.

"I'm so sorry," Lilly said softly.

"I am too." Naomi reached over and touched Susie's hand.

"*Danki*. I'm still sad sometimes, but mostly I try to be *froh*. I like to think of the fun my *mamm* and I had. We used to bake cookies and she would read me stories at bedtime." Susie picked up another cookie. "My *dat* said that Jesus needed my *mamm* and the *boppli*, and I'll see them again someday."

"That's right," Naomi said, forcing a smile. "You'll see them, and you can hug them again in heaven."

"Right." Susie's smile widened. "And I can tell them how much I love them." She sipped her water. "I loved watching my *mamm* when she quilted. I used to sit on a stool next to her and she'd teach me how to make the stitches. I loved all of the colors she used. My favorite quilts were the ones that had blues and maroons in them."

Naomi nodded. "I love those colors too. They look very *schee* together."

"I saw those at the farmers market," Susie said. "That's why I ran over to meet you. It reminded me of my *mamm*."

Overwhelmed by emotion, Naomi smiled. *The quilts and memories of her* mamm *are what drew her to me. It makes sense now.* "That's very nice, Susie. I'm so glad that you like my quilts."

"Will you teach me how to make a quilt?" Susie's eyes were filled with hope. "I really want to learn how."

"*Ya*," Naomi said. "If we have time during your visit, I would—"

"Susie!" Sadie yelled from across the room. "Susie, will you come here, please?"

Susie stood. "My *aenti* is calling me. I'll be back." She and Janie ran off to where Sadie stood with Irene Wagler, Miriam, and Sarah Rose.

Naomi turned to Lilly, whose eyes were wide with shock.

"That poor *kind*," Lilly whispered. "She's been through so much." She wiped her tearing eyes. "And her *mamm* was pregnant. I wonder what happened. How did she die?"

"I don't know," Naomi said. "I was wondering too."

She looked across the room. Sadie gave her a nasty look that seemed to say she should stay away, which sent a cold chill up Naomi's spine. Sadie then said something to Irene who glanced down at Susie and gave her a forced smile. She wondered what Sadie was saying, and for a split second she felt a pang of jealousy. She wanted to spend more time with Susie, but she pushed the thought away. Why should she feel any connection to a child who would soon return to her home in another state?

"What's on your mind, Naomi?" Lilly asked.

"Nothing." Naomi turned her attention back to the plate of cookies in front of her, but her appetite had evaporated after hearing the story of Susie's mother.

"You like her, don't you?" Lilly asked.

"What do you mean?"

"Susie," Lilly said. "You care about her."

"Of course I do," Naomi said simply. "She's a sweet little girl who lost her *mamm*. It's difficult not to care about her. I feel sorry for her."

"But you feel something deep for her," Lilly pressed on. "I can see it in your eyes. And she's attached to you as well."

Naomi avoided Lilly's stare by examining the crumbs on her plate. "Maybe Susie will want to write letters to me. Hopefully she will come to visit again soon."

"Naomi." Lilly touched her arm. "It's okay to say that you

care about the *kind* and want to get to know her better. Perhaps you should talk to her *dat*."

"What are you trying to get at?" Naomi asked with suspicion.

"You and the girl get along." Lilly shrugged. "Maybe the *dat* needs some company too after losing his *fraa*."

Naomi sighed. "We've discussed this. I'm not looking for love, and it's wrong to prey on a widower."

"Prey on him?" Lilly laughed. "How is it preying on him if you go and talk to him and tell him that you enjoy spending time with his *dochder*?"

Naomi glowered at her. "I know what you're thinking. You want me to try to court him, and I won't do it. I refuse to be called the *maedel* who runs after every eligible bachelor. My *mamm* called me that, and it didn't feel nice at all. Besides that, he's connected to the Kauffmans. I think it's time I give up on the Kauffman men. If I ever do court again, it will be a man who is in no way related to the Kauffmans. Maybe he won't even know the Kauffmans." She turned back to Susie, who was smiling up at Irene. "Please just drop it."

"Fine," Lilly said with a sigh. "But I have a feeling about this, Naomi. I can't shake the idea that you and Susie's *dat*—"

"Lilly," Naomi seethed. "Stop."

"Fine, fine." Lilly waved off the thought.

Naomi shook her head and wondered if Lilly could somehow be right about the connection Naomi felt toward Susie.

❧

Caleb climbed the steps to the bakery. "It feels like I was

just here yesterday," he said, glancing around the wraparound porch. "It looks the same as it did when we were kids."

"*Ya*, my *mamm* loves it and keeps it running with several of her daughters. We fix it up and repaint every spring." Timothy yanked the door open and they stepped into the bakery, which was bustling with women and girls who were laughing while straightening, sweeping, and cleaning.

"I guess we missed the party," Timothy said.

Caleb chuckled. "*Ya*, it sure looks like—"

"*Dat*!" Susie ran over, interrupting his words. "*Dat*!"

He bent down, and she wrapped her arms around him and kissed his cheek. Holding onto her, he closed his eyes and smiled. Oh, how he cherished his sweet little girl. "Did you have fun?" he asked.

"*Ya*!" She beamed. "I ate so many cookies! And I sat and talked to Naomi, my new *freind*." She pointed across the room to where Naomi stood with another young woman. "She's the one who makes the quilts at the farmers market." Taking his hand, Susie yanked him. "Come meet her."

"Okay," Caleb said. "Slow down."

Holding her hand, he followed her across the room. Naomi's gaze met his, and he was almost certain he glimpsed a flash of panic in her eyes before she glanced away. He wondered what that brief expression meant. Did his presence bother her?

"You'll like my new *freind*," Susie said, pulling Caleb toward Naomi.

"Caleb!" Sadie's voice called as she approached.

Caleb stepped toward Naomi, who looked up at him. As

he opened his mouth to speak to Naomi, Sadie stepped in front of him and grabbed his arm.

"I'm so glad you're here," Sadie said, turning him toward her. "Irene is here too. I know she would love to talk to you." She pushed him toward Irene, who stood with Sarah Rose Troyer and Rebecca Kauffman.

Susie grabbed his hand and tried to pull him backward. "*Dat*," she began with a huff, "I wanted you to meet *mei freind*."

"Susie," Caleb said, looking into her disappointed eyes. "I'll be just a moment."

"Irene was just telling me that her *dat* does have an opening for a new buggy mechanic," Sadie continued. "Right, Irene?"

Irene's smile was almost coy. "*Ya*, that's true, Caleb. I would be *froh* to introduce you."

"She's leaving!" Susie said. She stamped her foot and marched back toward Naomi.

Caleb opened his mouth to correct Susie's disrespectful display, but he didn't get a chance to speak. Instead, Irene continued chatting on about her father's shop, and Caleb wanted to interject. He waited for her to take a breath, but her words were strung together like a buggy wheel: no beginning, no end. He nodded, feigning interest, but his mind was set on a polite escape. He turned in the direction of Susie, and he spotted his daughter waving to Naomi as she headed out the front door with a woman about her age and three younger girls. He gave a sigh of defeat as he looked at Irene, who was still talking.

"I wanted you to meet *mei freind*," Susie said to Caleb while snuggling down in the bed next to her cousin later that evening.

"I know, but you were very disrespectful when you yelled and stamped your foot like a *boppli*." Caleb brushed a lock of brown hair back from Susie's forehead. "I'm certain I will talk to her before we leave."

"I'm sorry I acted like a *boppli*, but I was just disappointed. Naomi is really nice." Susie nodded with emphasis. "She said she's going to teach me to quilt."

Caleb smiled. "Is that so?"

"*Ya*." Susie glanced at Janie, who also nodded. "She's very pretty."

Ya, *she is*. He pushed that thought away.

"Tomorrow is the school program," Susie said. "I hope Naomi is there. Maybe you can meet her then."

He nodded. "Maybe so."

"Naomi will be there. Her sisters, Levina and Sylvia, go to the school. The Christmas program will be fun," Janie chimed in. "Susie is going to help us with the singing."

"That's *gut*." Caleb smiled at his niece. "It's time to get some sleep." Leaning over, he kissed Susie's cheek. "I'm glad you had fun today." He said good night to his nieces and then headed for the door.

As he descended the stairs, he contemplated Naomi. Susie was correct: Naomi was pretty. And he hoped his next encounter with the mysterious woman wasn't hijacked by his elder sister. In fact, he decided at that moment that he would make it a point to speak to the young woman who had his daughter so captivated.

CHAPTER 6

The following afternoon, Naomi shivered and pulled her cloak closer to her body while she trudged through the blowing snow from her family's buggy toward the one-room schoolhouse. Levina stumbled beside her, and Naomi grabbed her arm, steadying her younger sister on her feet as they moved through the swirling snow.

Irma, Naomi's mother, fell in step beside her. "I didn't think this snow was predicted for today. I thought the paper said the snow would start tomorrow."

Shaking her head, Naomi tightened her grip on her bag filled with treats and candies for the children who would perform the Christmas program. Each year, the teacher wrote the program, and the students practiced to get it just right. "No, I didn't think the snow was supposed to start before this evening."

Her brothers ran ahead, laughing and slipping through the snow.

"Slow down, boys," Titus, her father, bellowed. He shook his head. "They have such energy."

"*Ya*," Irma said, taking his hand. "They do. They get it from you." She gave Titus a sweet smile.

Naomi swallowed a sigh at the sweet sign of affection. She'd always admired the relationship her parents shared. She hoped that someday she'd find that kind of love and affection in a husband. She pushed the thought away since she believed in her heart that love wasn't in God's plan for her. Thinking about it too much would put her in a blue mood, and she needed to stay upbeat so she could enjoy the program.

A line of families moved slowly up the road through the snow toward the schoolhouse. Naomi couldn't help but think that the scene looked like a painting. The sky above them was gray, and the snow resembled a beautiful white fog engulfing the families who moved through it like apparitions dressed in dark cloaks and coats, some carrying gas lanterns, which glowed in the dark winter afternoon. The white, one-room schoolhouse was covered in the blowing snow, and buggies peppered with large, white flakes surrounded the little building.

They reached the schoolhouse at the end of the path, and Naomi shivered while stepping into the large room. A coal-burning stove provided warmth from the blustering cold afternoon. Rows of desks, benches, and folding chairs filled the center of the room, which was packed with children and their families. Paper snowflakes hung like mobiles fluttering from the ceiling, and drawings, including nativity scenes, angels, wreaths, and candles decked the walls. Similar drawings filled the blackboard at the front of the room. A makeshift curtain consisting of a few sheets hanging over twine hung at the front of the classroom in front of a raised platform that served as a stage next to the teacher's desk.

Naomi, Lizzie Anne, and her mother sat on an available

bench. Her father and Elam, her eldest brother at the age of nineteen, joined the men at the back of the room. Since Lizzie Anne had completed eighth grade last year, she'd graduated and was no longer a student at the school. Naomi greeted friends and chatted about the cold weather, while scanning the crowd consisting of members of her church district and families she'd known since her family moved to this district when she was sixteen, eight years ago.

Sylvia, Levina, and a group of their schoolmates hurried through the room, passing out handwritten pieces of paper with the schedule of program events, including Christmas-themed poems, songs, and skits. Naomi smiled, remembering her own happy memories of Christmas programs she'd participated in during eight years of school. She'd relished participating in the program with the other children. It was one of the highlights of every school year.

A mutter fell over the crowd and then the voices were silent.

"Good afternoon," Lena, the teacher, said. "*Danki* for coming to our program. The scholars have worked very hard, and we hope you enjoy it." She then glanced around the room. "Okay, *kinner*. Let's begin!"

The students lined up at the front of the classroom, the older children in back and the younger up front. Naomi spotted Susie standing with her cousins. When her gaze met Naomi's, she waved and grinned, and Naomi's heart warmed.

While children sang a round of Christmas carols, Naomi couldn't help but join in, as did many of the adults surrounding her. After the carols, the teacher rang a bell, and the children began acting out their skits and reciting their poems.

When Naomi's youngest brothers and group of friends presented impressions of their favorite animals, Naomi laughed and glanced at her smiling mother. She cut her eyes toward the men in the back of the room and found Caleb watching her, his eyes intense. With her cheeks blazing, Naomi turned back to the front of the room. She wished the sight of the widower didn't turn her insides to mush, but his eyes had mysterious power over her.

After several more skits, the program came to an end with another round of Christmas carols. The children invited the audience to join in, and Naomi tried to concentrate on the songs. However, her thoughts were focused on Caleb's intense green eyes and how they caused her body to warm.

As "Joy to the World" came to a close, the audience clapped and the children beamed.

Lena moved to the front of the room, her young face shining with a smile. *"Danki* for coming to our program," she said. "Please don't forget that Sadie Kauffman has invited us to come to her home for a little party. *Frehlicher Grischtdaag!"*

While conversations broke out around her, Naomi's stomach flip-flopped. She hoped she could convince her mother to skip the party in order to avoid more idle and awkward conversation with the Kauffmans.

Her mother leaned over. "I didn't know that we were going to Sadie's or I would've brought a covered dish."

Naomi shrugged. "Oh well. We can give out the candy and then head home. I'm sure the children are tired and—"

"Naomi." Her mother squeezed her hand. "It's Christmas. I'm certain Sadie will understand that we forgot a covered dish. It's about fellowship. The *kinner* will love being with their *freinden* a while longer."

Naomi shook her head, determined to avoid fellowship at Sadie's home. "*Ach*, I don't—"

"Naomi!" Susie rushed over and grabbed Naomi's sleeve. "I'm so *froh* you're here! I was hoping you'd see the program. Wasn't it great? What's your favorite Christmas carol? Mine is 'O Little Town of Bethlehem.' When I was little, I used to sing it all the time. How about you? Do you like to sing?"

Susie's father approached with a gentle smile. "Susie, you have to give her a chance to answer a question before you spout off six more."

The little girl giggled. "*Ya*, I guess you're right. Let's start with the most important question: What's your favorite Christmas carol?"

Although she was aware of Caleb's stare, Naomi kept her eyes on Susie. "My favorite is 'O Little Town of Bethlehem' too."

"That's *wunderbaar gut*! It was my *mamm's* too!" Susie grabbed Caleb's hand and yanked him closer. "This is my *dat*. His name is Caleb." She glanced up at her father. "*Dat*, this is *mei freind* Naomi I've been telling you about. She likes to quilt, bake, and sing, just like *Mamm* did!"

"It's nice to finally meet you, Naomi." His smile was warm as he held out his hand. "I've heard an awful lot about you."

With her heart in her throat, Naomi hesitated for a split second before taking his hand. The warm feel of his skin caused her breath to pause as her eyes locked with his.

"Are you coming over to my *Aenti* Sadie's house?" Susie asked, breaking the trance.

"Oh," Naomi said, pulling her hand back. "I don't know. I think I—"

"Please?" Susie's eyes were hopeful.

Naomi glanced up at Caleb.

"I think it's going to be a nice time," he said.

Nodding, Naomi finally gave in and smiled. "I'll be there after I help my *mamm* round up my siblings."

Gripping two mugs of Robert's homemade hot cider, Caleb weaved through the crowd in Sadie's family room for a second time and then back into the knot of people in the kitchen. He scanned the faces in search of Naomi's pretty smile. She'd seemed hesitant to join him and Susie at Sadie's house; however, she'd gathered up her siblings and steered them out the schoolhouse door and into the falling snow.

While her parents took their buggy to the house, Naomi and her siblings had walked the short distance from the schoolhouse to Sadie's home. He'd lost track of her amongst the group during the trek down the road toward Sadie's house, but he'd seen her younger sisters running around the house with Susie and a group of children. He hoped Naomi had chosen to stay with them. He was determined to speak to her for longer than that brief introduction they'd shared at the schoolhouse. He'd been captivated by her beautiful brown eyes and dimple while he'd watched her smiling and laughing during the children's program. Her warm handshake stirred something deep in his soul, a feeling he hadn't experienced since he'd lost Barbara.

When he spotted Naomi standing by the back door, his

steps quickened. She was still wearing her cloak, and he hoped she wasn't planning to hurry out the back door before they spoke again.

Moving toward her, he cleared his throat. "Naomi," he said, slipping between two laughing little boys.

"Oh, Caleb," she said. "Hi." Her cheeks flamed a bright pink. It seemed she was always blushing. He couldn't help but wonder if she always blushed in a man's presence. Whatever the reason, he found it adorable, and he was certain Naomi wasn't the temptress his sister had described.

"I hope you aren't planning on leaving." He held out one of the mugs. "I brought you some of Robert's famous hot cider. It's the best I've ever had."

"*Danki.*" She sipped from the cup and smiled. "*Ya*, it is *gut*. It's even better than my *dat's*, but I would never tell him that."

Caleb laughed. He opened his mouth to speak, but was interrupted by a group of young girls who ran by screeching through the kitchen on their way to the stairs leading to the second floor. Leaning in close to Naomi, he inhaled her flowery scent that must've been from her soap or shampoo. "Do you mind the cold?" he asked.

She shook her head. "Cold is fine."

"Want to go sit on the porch so we can hear each other speak?" He nodded toward the back door. "Then we don't have to compete with the *kinner*. I'm surprised Robert hasn't yelled for the *kinner* to keep it down, but I guess he knows he can't control the crowd."

"It is loud in here. Sitting outside sounds *gut*," she said.

He held the door open for her and followed her out onto

the sweeping, wraparound porch. She lowered herself onto a bench and shivered.

"Bad idea?" he asked.

She shook her head. "It's nice out here. The house was getting stuffy." She gestured toward the snowflakes dancing across the white pasture. "From the looks of those clouds, this snow may not stop any time soon."

"I think you're right." He sank onto the bench beside her and swallowed a shiver. He should've grabbed his coat from the peg by the door, but he was more focused on having an uninterrupted conversation with her than how he would weather the crisp December air. "We'll definitely have a white Christmas this year."

"Do you prefer white Christmases?" she asked before sipping from the mug.

"*Ya.*" He shrugged. He hadn't thought much about Christmas since he'd lost Barbara. "How about you?"

She mirrored his shrug. "*Ya.* I figure if it's going to be so cold, it might as well snow and make the scenery *schee* as a celebration of God's glory and our Savior's birth."

"I have to agree with that." He drank the hot cider and watched the snowflakes for a moment while trying to find a way to keep the conversation going. "What are your family Christmas traditions?"

"*Ach*, you know, nothing out of the ordinary." She set the mug down on the bench beside her. "We have the Christmas table with a place set for each of my siblings. I'm the oldest, and I love helping my mother set it up the night before. We put out little toys and candies for each of the *kinner*. I love seeing their faces Christmas morning. We have a big breakfast and then my *dat* sits in his favorite chair and tells the Christmas story from the book of Luke. It's *wunderbaar.* I look forward to it every year. How about you?"

Caleb studied the flakes that fluttered down onto the snow lining the wooden porch railing while he considered his answer. In all honesty, he and Susie hadn't really practiced any traditions since they'd lost Barbara. Last year, he gave her little gifts Christmas morning, and they'd placed a poinsettia on the mantle. But they didn't sing Christmas carols or share the Christmas story like they'd done when Barbara was alive. Beyond the Christmas program at school and a dinner shared with a neighbor, it seemed like just another day without Barbara.

"Susie and I don't really have any traditions anymore," he finally said. "We seem to just take things day by day with God's help."

Naomi's expression was sad. "I'm sorry for your loss." Her sweet voice was a mere whisper.

"I appreciate how nice you've been to my Susie," he said, placing his mug on the seat beside him. "You've taken a lot of time to talk with her, and not many adults seem to care enough to do that. *Danki.*"

Her smile and dimple were back. "Oh, it's nothing." She waved off the comment. "She's an easy girl to love."

"She's quite taken with you," he said, studying her eyes. "You seem to have a gift with *kinner.*"

Her cheeks were pink again, and he was certain it was more than just the cool breeze that colored them. "I've had a lot of experience with my siblings. My *mamm* once said I should've been a school teacher, but I thought quilting was the talent God wanted me to share." She paused as if gathering her thoughts. "Susie is a very special little girl. I've enjoyed spending time with her."

He nodded. "I believe she feels the same way about you. She's talked about you constantly since we met at the farmers market." He shook his head, embarrassed. "I'm sorry we made a scene that day."

"You didn't make a scene. It's scary when you think you've lost a *kind*. I took my siblings to the park one day last spring. My littlest brother, Joseph, was only four and wandered off while I was tying Leroy's shoe." She frowned. "I was scared to death with worry. There's a little stream that runs through the park, and I was certain he'd drowned." She laughed. "It turned out he was hiding behind a nearby tree, pretending to be a squirrel." Her expression was serious again. "But I understand how you felt at the farmers market. When you've lost sight of a child, your mind runs away with the most horrible possibilities of what could've happened to them."

The understanding in her pretty eyes touched him. "I feel like I've become even more protective of her since I lost Barbara," he said. "I guess it's because she's all I have left."

Naomi hugged her cloak closer to her body. "You must miss her so."

He nodded. "Every day."

"May I ask ...?" Her voice trailed off.

"What?" He rubbed his arms as the frosty air seeped into his skin. He wished he could run in and snatch his coat without losing a moment of conversation with Naomi.

"Nothing." She cleared her throat and glanced back toward the pasture. "The snow is beautiful, *ya*? I could watch it all night." She looked at his arms. "You should go get your coat. You don't want to spend your Christmas visit in bed or at the hospital with pneumonia, do you?"

"Naomi, you don't have to change the subject," he said with a smile. "You can ask me anything."

Standing, she pursed her lips. "You're going to catch a cold." She slipped in the door and returned a few moments later with a coat. "I grabbed one from of the peg by the door. It's my father's, but I don't think he'd mind if you borrowed it during our visit."

"*Danki.*" He pulled it on. Although the coat was a little large in the shoulders, it was warm. "What were you going to ask me?"

She bit her lower lip as if choosing her words. "I was wondering what happened to Barbara." She held a hand up, palm out. "But if it's too painful to share, I understand. I don't mean to pry into your life."

"It was Christmas Eve two years ago," he began, staring across the pasture. "We were so *froh* and excited back then. She was pregnant with our second *kind* and due at the end of January. Although she was feeling tired, she insisted that we celebrate with her cousins who lived on the other side of town. She'd baked a torte . . . Susie had helped her while they talked and laughed."

The memories flooded his mind like a rushing waterfall, with every detail bubbling forth, from the smell of her baked raspberry dream torte to the sight of her honey blonde hair sticking out from under her prayer *kapp*.

"I'd wanted to stay home because Barbara said that she had some back pain, but she'd insisted we go," he continued, lifting the mug of cider. "She'd even invited our neighbors to join us, and looking back, I'm certain she did to give herself an excuse to go no matter what." He chuckled to himself. "Barbara was good at that—finding ways to get what she wanted. Not that she was deceitful. She had a heart of gold. She knew our neighbors were celebrating Christmas alone that year, and she wanted to give them *froh* memories."

"She was very caring," Naomi said softly.

"*Ya*, she was." He glanced over at her, and her lip twitched as her eyes filled with tears. He hoped she didn't cry. He didn't want to cause her any sadness while they visited together. He also didn't want to cry and show too much emotion in front of her and seem as if he were weak.

"We'd spent all afternoon with her cousins and had a *gut* time," he said. "We ate too much, and the *kinner* played well together while sharing their Christmas candy and toys. We stayed much later than we should've, but Susie was having so much fun with her cousins."

He sipped the cider and looked back over the pasture as the memories of that tragic night gripped him.

"On the way home, I was riding in a buggy behind her and witnessed the whole thing." His voice quavered. He cleared his throat before continuing. "Barbara had wanted to ride back to our house with our neighbor and her family. For some reason, Susie insisted on riding with me. She said she was afraid I would get lost if I rode home alone." He snorted at the irony.

"She's such a thoughtful *kind*," Naomi whispered, wiping a tear.

"A pickup truck ran a red light and ..." His voice trailed

off as the graphic images of the crash flooded his mind. He shook the memories away. "My neighbor and her family suffered bruises and scrapes. But my Barbara and our unborn baby took the brunt of the impact." His voice fell to a whisper. "They were killed instantly."

"I'm so sorry." Tears glistened in Naomi's brown eyes. "I can't imagine how difficult it was for you and Susie."

He wiped his eyes, hoping to prevent any threatening tears from splashing down his cheeks. "The month that followed her death was a blur. Of course, God was with me the whole time, and I believe He still is." He paused and pulled at his beard while gathering his thoughts. "To be honest, the most difficult part has been the day-to-day routine, the things we do without thinking twice. You know, getting Susie ready for school, making her lunch, combing her hair, going to bed alone at night. That's when I miss Barbara the most."

Naomi wiped her eyes again. "That would make sense. You miss her the most when you're alone with Susie or just plain alone."

He nodded, impressed by her understanding of his loss. "That's it exactly. It's funny how your life can change in a split second. One minute I was riding down a road thinking about how much fun I'd had at the little party and listening to my little girl chatter endlessly about Christmas. Then the next moment I was trying to hold my emotions together while I held my little girl at the scene of the accident."

"Life does have a tendency to change on us in a split second," Naomi said, holding her mug in her hands.

He raised his eyebrow. "You sound like you speak from experience."

She shrugged while studying the contents of the mug. "I've made plans that haven't turned out the way I'd thought. Of course, it's nothing like you've experienced. My heartaches have been on a much smaller scale."

"Your heartaches?" he asked, his curiosity piqued. "Do you want to share?"

Naomi shook her head. "I'd rather not. It's just silliness." She sipped more of her drink. "This is the best cider I've ever tasted. Makes me thirsty for Robert's summer root beer. It's especially tasty with some vanilla ice cream."

"*Ya*, it is good. We'll have to do that next time we come visit," he said. "Susie and I will be sure to have the floats ready."

She gave him a surprised expression. "Okay."

He studied her eyes, wishing he could read her thoughts. "I've talked your ear off," he said. "Tell me about your life here in Bird-in-Hand."

She shrugged and cleared her throat. "It's nothing out of the ordinary. You already know that I work at the quilt stand in the farmers market and I help care for my siblings."

"What do you like to do for fun?" he asked, crossing his ankle onto his knee.

She laughed. "For fun?"

"That's right." He nodded. "You have fun, right?"

"Hmm." She gnawed her bottom lip and hugged her cloak closer to her body. "I enjoy reading with my youngest siblings. Leroy and Joseph are learning quickly how to sound out words." Her fingers moved to the ties of her black bonnet, and she absently moved them on her chin. "I love to quilt, and we sometimes have quilting bees." She turned to him, her eyes full of excitement. "In fact, we're having one here tomorrow, and I hope Susie will attend. She's asked me to teach her to quilt, and I'd love to give her some instructions."

He grinned. "She'd love that."

"*Gut.*" She smiled. "I guess that's about it."

"So everything you enjoy is for someone else?"

She laughed. "I guess so. But isn't that what God has instructed us to do—to give of ourselves?"

"*Ya*, He has." Caleb wondered why she wasn't married yet. He surmised she was in her mid-twenties. Why hadn't some eligible bachelor swooped her up?

She gestured toward the front door. "You grew up here, *ya*?"

"I did."

"What took you to Ohio?"

"Love." He folded his arms across his chest. "I met Barbara while she was visiting her cousin here one summer. We courted through letters and the phone for a while, and I made a couple of trips up to visit her. She didn't want to leave her *mamm*, who was alive when we first met, so I moved there."

"Are many of Barbara's relatives still there?"

He shook his head. "No, just a handful of cousins in neighboring church districts."

"What do you do for a living?" she asked.

"I'm a buggy maker."

"Do you ever miss living here?"

He nodded. "Sometimes I do. Sometimes I wish I'd convinced Barbara to come live here, but when I think about that too much, I make myself *narrisch*, wondering if she'd still be alive. Then again, it's not our place to question God's will, is it?"

Naomi shook her head. "No, it's not." She then tilted her

head in question, her eyes thoughtful. "Do you believe that God only gives us one chance at true love? Or do you think He provides us the opportunity to love more than once during a lifetime?"

"That is a very *gut* question." He idly rubbed his beard while considering his answer. "I would say that God gives us second chances. I think Timothy's youngest sister is a great example of that." He was almost certain he saw her flinch at the mention of his best friend's name.

"*Ya,*" she said softly. "That is a *gut* point."

Her eyes were full of something that seemed to resemble regret or possibly grief. He wanted to ask her what had happened to her to make her so sad, but the back door opened with a whoosh, revealing Sadie. Did his sister have a sixth sense when it came to ruining perfect moments?

"Caleb!" Sadie exclaimed, her face full of shock. "What are you doing out here in the cold?" She turned to Naomi and her eyes narrowed slightly, looking annoyed. "Oh, Naomi. *Wie geht's?*"

"I'm fine, *danki.*" Naomi rose and stepped toward the door. "How are you?"

"Fine, fine. You must come in out of this cold before you both get sick." Sadie motioned for Naomi to enter the house. As Naomi stepped through the doorway, she shot Caleb a quizzical expression as if to ask what he'd been doing on the porch with Naomi. "That's not your coat, is it?" she asked.

Caleb stood and shook his head. "No, this coat belongs to Naomi's *dat.* She grabbed it for me when I started shivering."

Once Naomi was through the door, Sadie stepped back

onto the porch and closed the door. "What are you doing out here, Caleb?"

"Just talking with my new *freind*." He moved past her. "We were discussing the snow and Christmas." He shrugged. "That was all."

She took his arm and pulled him toward the door. "I have plenty of families I want you to meet, so you must come back inside."

"Yes, *schweschder*." He forced a smile and she steered him through the door. As he walked by Naomi and her mother, Caleb rolled his eyes and then smiled. Naomi laughed, and he gave her a little wave.

Sadie guided Caleb toward Irene Wagler who stood with her father and another couple. Caleb nodded a greeting and then glanced back at Naomi, who blushed and looked away.

"Caleb," Sadie said with a sweeping gesture, "this is Hezekiah Wagler, Irene's father."

Caleb shook the middle-aged gentleman's hand. "It's nice to meet you."

"You too," Hezekiah said. "I hear you are a buggy maker. I've owned my own shop for thirty years."

While the man began to describe his shop, Caleb glanced toward Naomi standing with her mother, and his mind wandered back to their conversation on the porch. He wished he could've sat with Naomi for much longer, perhaps hours, while they continued their conversation. She was so beautiful and so easy to talk to and he felt a connection to her, as if she could be a kindred spirit.

While he missed Barbara so much his heart ached some days, he felt something new when he looked at Naomi. She ignited a glimmer of hope that he might somehow find love again. Although he could never replace Barbara, he suddenly wondered if he could find happiness and build a life with a woman as special as Naomi. He had the suspicion he could love again, and Naomi King could possibly hold that key.

A smile turned up the corner of Caleb's lips. The possibility of finding a life mate again filled him with a joy he hadn't felt in years. He looked forward to exploring that future, but he knew he had to move slowly and make sure it was right. He didn't want to do anything to hurt Susie or Naomi.

Caleb turned back to the Waglers, and Sadie shot him a curious look.

Ignoring his sister, Caleb continued to smile and nod while Hezekiah discussed his booming business. He tried his best to look interested and engaged in the discussion, even though his thoughts were on the other side of the room with Naomi.

Caleb would keep his excitement about his evolving feelings for Naomi King to himself and let God lead him. He believed that with God, all things were possible, even the potential of a widower finding love again.

CHAPTER 7

The word *quilting* refers to the hand stitching of three layers: a pieced top, a layer of batting, and a bottom fabric layered together, then stitched together in a pattern to hold the layers together," Naomi began while holding up a quilt and showing it to Susie the following morning while they stood together in Sadie's kitchen.

Deep in thought, Susie scrunched her nose and swiped her hand over the cream, blue, and maroon quilt created in a log cabin pattern.

"See here?" Naomi ran her hand over the pattern. "The top layers were pieced together on the treadle sewing machine I have at my house in my room. The quilting is always done by hand. Then a binding is sewn onto the bottom layer by the machine and hand stitched to the top layer." She smiled at Susie's little tongue, sticking out of her mouth as if she were contemplating the meaning of life. "I'm sure you already know that we use what the Englishers consider an old-fashioned sewing machine powered by a pedal and no electricity." She felt her admiration for the little girl growing by the minute.

Naomi had arrived at Sadie's that morning along with

her sisters, mother, and Lilly. As soon as Naomi stepped in the door, Susie ran over and began chatting without taking a breath—asking question after question about Naomi's quilt, which she held in her hands. Naomi brought it in order to explain how a quilt was created.

While Naomi was excited to spend time with Susie, she couldn't help but be disappointed that Caleb had already left for a day of visiting his friends and acquaintances in town. She'd spent all evening thinking about their conversation on the porch.

Throughout the night, she'd tossed and turned, analyzing his words and remembering the sadness in his eyes while he'd discussed his beloved wife. She knew that she was developing feelings for the man, and she wished she could suppress them. However, her stomach fluttered at the thought of seeing him and speaking to him again.

Susie ran her hand over the stitching. "You sewed the top layer and then you hand stitched it all together?"

"That's right." Naomi nodded toward the family room where the women sat around a frame that held Sadie's latest creation. "See how all the women are stitching that quilt your *aenti* made? My *mamm* and I stitched this one. Since it's only a twin size, we didn't need a whole group to help us."

Susie studied the creation in her hands. "Who did you make this one for?"

Naomi shrugged. "This one was really just for fun. I was experimenting with the colors. Do you like it?"

Susie's eyes were bright. "I love it."

Naomi smiled. Perhaps the quilt could be a surprise Christmas gift for her little friend. She gestured toward the family room. "Did you want to go help the women with that quilt your *aenti* is finishing for the English customer?"

"No. Let's talk instead." Susie sat on a kitchen chair. "Did you have any of my *onkel's* cider last night?"

Naomi sat across from her. "I did. It was *appeditlich*."

The little girl nodded. "*Ya*, it was *wunderbaar*. I told my *dat* he needs to learn how to make cider like that."

Naomi laughed while standing. "That would be nice, wouldn't it?"

Susie tilted her head in question. "Do you believe in Christmas miracles, Naomi?"

Naomi's smile faded as she crossed the kitchen, grabbed two cups of water, and brought them over to the table. "Sure, Susie. Why do you ask?"

"*Danki*," Susie said, taking the cup. "Janie and Linda said that one of their cows was born on Christmas Eve last year, and their *dat* said it was a miracle because it was so cold." She sipped her water.

"I imagine it was a miracle." Naomi sipped the water, wondering where this conversation was headed.

Susie glanced toward the women in the family room next to the kitchen and then moved closer to Naomi. "May I tell you a secret?" she whispered.

"Of course," Naomi said softly, leaning closer to her.

"There's a Christmas miracle I've been praying for." Susie wiggled her chair closer to Naomi. "My dream is for my *dat* to be *froh* again on Christmas. I want to see him smile. I mean really smile. He smiles now, but I don't think he's truly *froh* since *Mamm* is gone. I want him to be really and truly *froh*."

Naomi smiled as tears filled her eyes. "That's very sweet, Susie."

"Do you think it's possible?" Susie asked, still whispering. "Do you think God will grant me that one miracle?"

Naomi pushed a lock of hair that had escaped Susie's prayer covering away from her face. "With God, all things are possible," she whispered.

"What are you two scheming?" Sadie asked, stepping into the kitchen and shooting Naomi a suspicious expression.

"We're just talking, *Aenti* Sadie," Susie said. "Naomi was telling me all about quilts."

Sadie grabbed a stack of dishes from the cabinet. "I thought you wanted to learn how to make them. If you want to learn how, then you need to come join us in the *schtupp* and not sit out here gabbing with Naomi."

Naomi bit her bottom lip to hold back the stinging retort she wanted to throw back at Sadie. Why did Sadie have to nag Susie when they were having a nice time together?

"Let's serve lunch, Susie," Sadie said.

Naomi and Susie helped Sadie spread out the food for lunch, including chicken salad, homemade bread, pickles, and meadow tea. The women gathered around the table. After a silent prayer, they discussed their upcoming Christmas plans while eating.

Naomi was filling the sink with soapy water for the dirty dishes when the back door opened and shut with a bang. She spotted Caleb following Robert into the family room, and her stomach flip-flopped. She was glad that Irene Wagler hadn't come to the quilting bee. Although she knew it was a sin, she couldn't ignore the jealousy she'd felt when Caleb had spoken to Irene and Irene's father last night. She'd felt a special connection with Caleb during their conversation on the porch. She knew that she had no future with the widower since he and his daughter would soon return to Ohio. However, she couldn't stop the growing attraction that bubbled up in her every time she saw him.

"*Dat*!" Susie rushed over and hugged Caleb, nearly knocking him over. "We've had such fun!" She began rattling off details of her new knowledge of quilt-making.

Grinning, Caleb shucked his coat and hung it on the peg by the door. Turning, he met Naomi's stare, and her pulse skittered. She looked back toward the sink and began scrubbing the dirty utensils as a diversion from his captivating eyes.

Conversations swirled around her while she continued washing the dirty serving platters and bowls. A tug on her apron caused her to jump with a start. She glanced down at Susie smiling up at her.

"Naomi?" Susie asked, her big green eyes hopeful. "My *dat* and I were wondering if you would go shopping with us."

"Shopping?" Naomi wiped her hands on a dish towel as she faced Susie and Caleb.

Sadie stepped behind Caleb and studied her brother. "Shopping?" she echoed. "Where are you going shopping?"

He shrugged. "Susie wants to go Christmas shopping, and it sounds like fun to fight the crowds. I don't care where we go. I'll leave the location up to Susie and Naomi."

"Will you come with us?" Susie grabbed Naomi's arm and tugged. "There are some things I want to get for my cousins."

Sadie gave Naomi a hard look, and Naomi paused. She

knew how Sadie relished sharing gossip at her quilting bees, and that was the reason why Naomi had enjoyed staying in the kitchen with Susie instead of listening to Sadie's latest news.

Naomi met Susie's hopeful eyes and silently debated what to do. She didn't want to hurt the little girl's feelings, but she also knew the possible consequences. Going shopping alone with Caleb and his daughter could start rumors that would upset Naomi's mother.

"Well, I don't know." Naomi turned back to the sink. "There are an awful lot of dishes to be cleaned up, and then I need to help finish the quilt. Sadie has a customer who is going to pick it up tomorrow since it's a Christmas gift for her daughter."

"I'll help finish the dishes," Caleb said, grabbing a dish towel.

Stunned, Naomi stared at him. "You will?"

He chuckled. "Believe it or not, I cook and do dishes back home."

"I just don't know." Naomi felt Sadie's scrutinizing stare. "I think I need to stay and help with the quilt."

Susie frowned. "Are you certain?"

Once Sadie had walked away, Caleb sidled up to Naomi and began to dry a serving platter. "Would you feel more comfortable if one of your sisters or perhaps one of my nieces came along with us?" he asked her under his breath.

Naomi studied him, wondering how this man could read her mind. "How did you know?"

He gave a small smile. "I know how *mei schweschder* works."

Naomi leaned closer to him. She couldn't help but inhale his manly scent, like earth mixed with a spicy deodorant. "What do you mean?" she asked.

He placed the dry platter on the counter. "She had spread the news about my proposal to Barbara before I had even decided to propose. She should've been an editor for the local paper instead of a quilt maker." He snatched a handful of clean utensils from the sink. "I'll finish the dishes, and Susie can help me put them away. Why don't you see if one of your sisters or my nieces wants to join us? That will quell any rumors about our shopping expedition."

"Are you certain?" Naomi placed the dish towel on the counter.

"I'm drying the dishes, aren't I?" he asked with a grin.

She couldn't help but smile. His handsome face was nearly intoxicating. "*Danki.*"

"No need to thank me," he said, opening the utensil drawer. "You're going to help me more than you know. Shopping is not one of my strengths."

CHAPTER 8

Caleb walked through the flea market with Naomi by his side while Susie, her cousin Janie, and Naomi's sisters, Levina and Sylvia, skipped ahead toward a candy concession stand.

The ride over to the indoor flea market in Robert's borrowed buggy had been noisy, with the four girls chatting all at once in the back seat. Caleb had stolen several glances at Naomi and found her fingering the ties on her black bonnet and the hem of her cloak. He wondered what she was thinking and if she was enjoying her time with him as much as he enjoyed his time with her.

"How come we haven't met before now?" he asked, falling into step with her while holding the bags containing a few small gifts he'd picked up for Sadie and Robert.

She gave him a confused expression. "Excuse me?"

"You didn't go to school with the Kauffmans, right?" he asked.

She shook her head. "No. I grew up in a district that's a few miles away. My *dat* decided to move to a larger farm when I was sixteen." She paused, gathering her thoughts. "You're close to the Kauffmans, *ya*?"

He nodded. "Timothy's been my best *freind* for as long as I can remember."

"Oh." She frowned.

"You don't like the Kauffmans much, do you?" He felt like a liar for asking the question. He knew part of the answer since Timothy had shared that he'd broken Naomi's heart. However, he wanted to hear her version of her past with Timothy and Luke. He knew in his gut that Sadie was wrong about Naomi. She seemed like a quiet, honest young woman, not a woman who was too eager to find a husband.

"It's not that." Her cheeks were pink again. "I just. *Ach.* I sort of—"

"Naomi!" Levina's loud voice interrupted Naomi. "Can I have some money? I want to get some licorice."

"Oh." Naomi pulled out her small black handbag.

"I got it." Caleb touched her warm hand and then pulled out his wallet.

"Oh no." Naomi shook her head. "That's not necessary. I don't expect you to buy candy for my sisters."

"It's my pleasure." He handed Levina a ten. "Please buy for all of the girls."

"*Danki*, Caleb." Levina smiled and trotted off to the candy counter.

"*Danki*," Naomi said.

"*Gern gshehne.*" He motioned toward a bench near the candy stand. "Let's sit for a moment. What were you saying about the Kauffmans?"

She smoothed her skirt. "It's rather embarrassing."

"I'm certain it can't be that bad."

She frowned and placed her plain, black handbag on her lap. "I'd rather not talk about it."

"That's fine," he said, glancing toward the girls, who were busy ordering candy at the stand. "What do you want for Christmas?"

"Me?" Naomi laughed. "*Ach*, I don't need anything."

He studied her deep brown eyes. "There must be something you'd like. There's always something we don't need that we'd like to have, even if it's considered unnecessary or frivolous."

"Well." She tapped her chin and glanced toward a bookstand. "There's a pretty Bible that I looked at a few weeks ago. I'm still waiting for it to go on sale. The binding on my Bible is falling apart, but I don't necessarily need a new one. However, every night when I open it for my devotional time, I feel the fraying binding and think about how nice it would be to have a new one."

"Interesting." He smiled. "You'll have to show it to me before we leave."

Naomi shrugged. "Alright. So what about you? What do you want for Christmas?"

At first he waved off the question because he couldn't think of anything he wanted. But then the answer hit him like a speeding, oncoming freight train. The truth was that he did want something, and it was as if a light bulb went off in his head and in his heart. The feeling was overwhelming and it was brand new, something he hadn't felt in a long, long time. What he wanted for Christmas was something he'd probably never experience again. He wanted a companion. Someone to share his life with. Someone to tell his hopes and dreams to and to help him through the tough times. Someone to help him raise Susie in a faithful Christian home.

He wanted a life partner.

He wanted a wife and a mother for Susie.

But finding that wasn't as easy as Sadie had made it sound.

Besides, worrying about his own needs was selfish and self-serving, since he knew his focus had to be on being the best parent he could for Susie. Aside from God, she was the center of his life now. Concentrating on finding a new wife would only take his focus away from Susie, which would be wrong.

Therefore, he couldn't tell Naomi the truth about what he wanted for Christmas because it was too embarrassing.

"I don't need anything." Grinning, he raised an eyebrow. "Sound familiar?"

She mirrored his grin, and she was adorable. "There must be *something* you want, no matter how unnecessary and frivolous it may sound, Caleb. Isn't that what you told me?"

He glanced across the large flea market toward a booth with antique tools they'd passed earlier. "There was a tool I spotted over there that would be a great one to add to my collection, but it's nothing I necessarily need."

She touched his hand. "I'll make a deal with you. I'll show you my dream Bible if you show me that tool you want but don't need."

He shook her hand. "It's a deal."

Her smile was bright, revealing her dimple. "*Wunderbaar.*"

"*Dat,*" Susie asked, approaching them. "Can we get some fudge?"

Caleb glanced at Naomi, and she shrugged while pulling

out her wallet. "Let me pay this time. You paid for the licorice."

He leaned close to her and inhaled her flowery scent, wondering briefly if it was her shampoo. "Put your money away," he whispered. He then turned to Susie. "That's a *gut* idea. Let's all get some fudge."

Stepping over to a fudge stand, he ordered a slab for the girls and then some for himself and Naomi.

"You're much too generous," Naomi said before breaking off a piece from the small block. "I could've paid for my sisters and me."

He shook his head. "Don't be *gegisch*. It was just fudge."

"*Danki*," she said.

He wished he could get her to open up to him, but he didn't want to push her. He and Susie would head back to Ohio soon, so any thoughts of a relationship would be preposterous. Yet, he was captivated by her.

She smiled and then nodded toward the girls, who were disappearing in the crowd. "We'd better catch up to them."

He nodded. "You're right."

They weaved through a knot of shoppers and caught up with the girls at a toy stand.

"Did you have a nice day in town today?" she asked.

"*Ya*," he said. "I ran some errands with Robert and visited some old *freinden*."

"I bet your friends were *froh* to see you," she said, wiping her mouth with a napkin.

"I think so." He shrugged while biting into the chocolate. "We stopped by the Kauffman Furniture store so Robert could talk to his *dat* and brothers." He shook his head as he recalled the conversations. "Timothy and his brothers are mounting a campaign to get me to move back here. They were trying to get me to go visit a shop that's for sale near the furniture store."

"Oh?" Her eyes rounded with interest. "Did you go visit it?"

He shook his head. "Not yet. But I might."

The girls sat on a bench outside the toy stand and giggled while eating their fudge, and Caleb wondered if he should go visit the shop owner. Would moving Susie closer to his family be a way to help her heal after losing her mother?

He motioned toward a bench near the girls. "Should we sit and finish our chocolate?"

"That's a *gut* idea." Naomi sat down. "I didn't mean to be rude before."

"Rude?" He sank down next to her. "What do you mean?"

"When you asked me what I thought of the Kauffmans." She studied her remaining square of fudge, and he wondered if she was avoiding his eyes. "It's just that I've made some mistakes that I regret, and they aren't easy to talk about."

Guilt rained down on him for pushing her to discuss it. He didn't want to make her uncomfortable. "You don't have to tell me. It's none of my business."

"No," she said, frowning as she looked up at him. "You've been honest with me, so I need to be honest with you. Timothy and I courted for a short while, but we broke up when we realized that we weren't right for each other. I also courted Luke Troyer for a short time. *Mei mamm* said I was too eager with them, and I know she's right." Her cheeks blazed a bright pink, and he wished he could ease her embarrassment. "But I was young then. I'm almost twenty-five and I know better now. I won't rush into another relationship. In fact, I think God would prefer I help *mei mamm* raise my siblings rather than court."

He raised an eyebrow in surprise. "Don't you think you're being a bit too hard on yourself? We've all had our hearts broken at one time or another, but God still wants us to get married and have a family. You said yourself that God can give us a second chance at love."

She shook her head. "That's not what I said. I asked you if *you* believe God gives us a second chance, but I never said I believe it."

"But you agreed that God gave Sarah Rose a second chance with Luke."

"*Ya*, I did," she said softly. "But I'm not so sure he'd be willing to give me a third chance."

"What makes you think God puts a cap on how many chances we can have to find love?"

Naomi looked away from his stare. "I don't know. It's just a feeling I have."

"You're young," Caleb said. "Don't give up on love so quickly. Barbara had an *onkel* who didn't marry until he was almost fifty. He never gave up on love."

She gasped. "Really? He was almost fifty?"

"I'm not saying you'll have to wait that long," he added, wiping his beard with a napkin. "I would imagine you'll be snatched up quickly with that *schee* smile of yours."

Looking embarrassed, she bit into the fudge. He wondered what on earth Timothy did to shatter her heart into pieces. Timothy had hinted that he wasn't proud of how their relationship had ended. He must not have let her down too easily.

They ate in silence for a few moments. The girls finished their fudge, and Susie came over and got money from Caleb in order to purchase a few small toys. While the girls shopped, Caleb and Naomi finished their chocolate.

"How about we go into that antique place?" she asked, wiping her mouth. "I want to see that tool you need."

He took her used napkin from her and tossed it into the trash along with his. "You forgot what I said. I don't *need* it. I would like to have it."

She grinned as she stood. "I meant to say, show me the tool that you *would like* to have."

"That's right." They walked over to the toy shop together, and he approached the girls. "We'll be right next door looking at the antiques. When you're finished shopping, come over and join us."

The girls agreed, and he and Naomi entered the antique shop, where he led her over to the tools. Her eyes widened as she glanced over the assortment of gadgets.

"Wow," she said. "Are these the tools you use for your buggy projects?"

He grinned. "No, I actually use modern tools, but I like to collect antiques. I can use them, and sometimes I do. But mostly, I collect them for fun."

She picked up an antique saw and studied it as if it were a precious piece of glass. "How did you start your collection?"

He picked up a hand drill. "My *grossdaddi* started the collection. Actually, he used the tools in his carriage shop. I like to add to it every now and then. It's not really a frivolous expense because I can actually use them." He turned the drill over in his hand, examining the craftsmanship.

"Is that the one you want?" she asked as she stepped over to him.

Caleb nodded. "*Ya*. Like I said, I don't need it, but it would be nice to have." He placed it back on the counter. "I guess we should go find the girls and see if my *dochder* is finished spending my money yet."

"Are women ever finished spending a man's money?" Naomi's smile was coy.

He grinned. "If I answer that question truthfully, will I get smacked?"

She tapped her chin, feigning deep thought. "I don't know. I suppose it depends on the answer."

He laughed and suppressed the urge to put his arm around her shoulders and pull her in to his arms for a hug. He enjoyed her easy sense of humor. Spending time with her was akin to relaxing, a feeling he hadn't enjoyed in months—no, more like years.

"*Dat*!" Susie rushed over, her three shopping bags rustling against her cloak. "I think I'm finished. I got some candy and toys. Want to see?" She held open one of the bags and found a plethora of lollipops, chocolate coins, ring pops, candy canes, marbles, small rubber balls, and little toy cars.

"Very nice, Susie." He touched her cheek. "I think you're going to make your *freinden* and cousins very happy on Christmas."

"Are we heading home now?" Katie asked. "I think I have to help my *mamm* start supper."

"*Ya*," Caleb said, placing his hand on Susie's shoulder. "I believe your *dat* may send out a search party if we don't head home soon." He glanced at Naomi. "You need to show me that Bible you were talking about earlier before we head out."

"*Ach*, it's not something I need." Naomi waved it off as they weaved through the crowd.

Levina sidled up to Naomi and took her hand. "That pretty Bible you always visit when you come in here?"

Naomi swung her sister's hand and smiled down at her. "It's not something I need. I can still enjoy God's Word with the Bible I have."

Caleb smiled at the tenderness between the sisters and he took Susie's hand. "We'll stop at the book store on the way out."

They entered the little book stand, and he followed her over to a display of Bibles.

Sylvia pointed to a plain but elegant black Bible. "This is the one she wants."

Naomi's cheeks were pink again. "But I really don't need it."

Caleb glanced at the price tag. "Would you want your name engraved on the front?"

Naomi shook her head. "Oh, it's just too much. I couldn't expect you to—"

"*Ya*, she does," Levina chimed in. "*Mamm* and *Dat* have one that was engraved for them on their wedding day, and Naomi has always thought that was a nice gift. She said she wants one with her name on it too."

"Levina," Naomi gently scolded. "You need to mind your own business."

Janie glanced toward the clock on the wall. "We better go," she said, starting toward the door. "I don't want my *dat* angry with me. You know how he gets."

Caleb nodded, knowing how short his brother-in-law's temper could be. He distinctly remembered the early years of Sadie's marriage to Robert, when he'd yell at her for things as simple as supper not being ready at his requested time.

Once the girls were loaded into the back of the buggy, Caleb climbed into the buggy seat next to Naomi. "Do you want me to drop you and your sisters off at home?"

She nodded. "That would be *wunderbaar.*"

While the girls chatted about snow and Christmas, Caleb and Naomi rode in silence. He wondered if she'd had as much fun as he'd had today. He wished the afternoon didn't have to end. The idea of moving back to Bird-in-Hand swirled through his mind. Should he go look at that shop? Should he make an offer on the place if it was a good deal? Did he want to uproot Susie? Was he entitled to the happiness he could possibly have here in Lancaster County?

Out the corner of his eye, he spotted his daughter laughing with her cousin and Naomi's sisters. If he moved her here, he wouldn't so much as uproot her as give her a sense of family. Surely, she would miss her friends back in Ohio, but she would also make new friends, including Naomi's sisters and Naomi herself.

"Turn here," Naomi said, breaking through his thoughts. "Then go about half a mile and turn right."

"Oh," Caleb said with a smile. "You're not far at all from Sadie's house."

Naomi shook her head. "Just a little ways, really."

"Close enough to walk," he said, steering around a corner.

"*Ya,*" she said, lifting her purse from the floorboard. "I think Susie got all that she wanted today."

"I think so," he said.

She pointed toward a large, white farmhouse. "That's it."

"*Danki* for coming," he said as he steered toward her driveway.

"*Danki* for the invitation," she said, turning toward him. "I had a nice time."

"I did too." And he hoped that they could get together again sometime soon.

"Let's go, girls," Naomi said, facing her sisters. "We have to get started on supper." She opened the door, hopped down from the buggy, and helped her sisters down. After saying good-bye to the girls in the back, Naomi turned to Caleb. "Have a nice evening."

"You too," he said. "I hope to see you again soon."

She smiled. "*Ya*, I do too." She said good-bye to the girls and then hurried toward the house with her sisters in tow.

As Caleb steered toward Sadie's house, he decided he needed to check into that shop that Timothy had recommended, and an unfamiliar excitement filled him.

CHAPTER 9

"Go wash up," Naomi told her siblings as she set the table later that evening. "Supper is almost ready."

The children filed out of the kitchen, and Naomi lined the plates up on the long table.

Her mother placed a large bowl of mashed potatoes at the center of the table. "Did you have fun today?"

"*Ya*," Naomi said, snatching a handful of utensils from the drawer. "Susie wanted to shop for Christmas gifts for her cousins and friends. She, Janie, Sylvia, and Levina had a *gut* time shopping, and Caleb and I just walked around and talked."

"What did you and Caleb discuss?" Irma began to fill a platter with homemade rolls.

"Oh, nothing much." Naomi lined the utensils up by the place settings. "We talked about Christmas and things like that. He's very easy to talk to. We had a nice time together." She didn't want to admit they'd talked about her doomed relationships.

Irma gave Naomi a hard look, and Naomi wished she hadn't even mentioned Caleb's name.

Rather than argue about Naomi's track record with

dating, Naomi decided to change the subject. "How did the quilt turn out? Did you get it finished before the customer arrived?"

Irma placed the platter next to the rolls and glowered. "I hope you're not getting any ideas about this widower, Naomi. You know he's going back to Ohio after the holidays and you're just going to get your heart broken if you get too attached."

Naomi breathed out a deep sigh. "*Mamm*, I know that. He's just a *freind*."

Her mother continued to frown. "Don't make a fool of yourself again. You never should've gone out with him today. You know how that will look to the rest of the community."

"He invited me," Naomi said, pointing to her chest. "It wasn't my idea. In fact, I think it was Susie's idea. She really likes me, and I enjoy spending time with her too. You know she lost her *mamm* only two years ago. For some reason, she's latched on to me, and how can I turn her away?"

Irma wagged a finger at Naomi. "You can't be her *mamm*. That's not your place."

"I never said I wanted to be her mother. I just want to be her *freind*. Is that so wrong?"

"*Ach*, no." Irma shook her head. "But I know you, Naomi. You get too attached, and that will only lead to trouble."

Naomi shook her head. "I can't do anything right in your eyes, can I, *Mamm*? The way you see it, I mess up completely when it comes to love, and I'm destined to be alone."

"I wasn't speaking of love," Irma said, pulling the broccoli and rice casserole from the oven. "I was talking about perceptions. It just didn't look right for you to go out shopping with that widower and his *dochder*. It looked very inappropriate, and you know how people talk."

"I don't see how any of my behavior was inappropriate, *Mamm*." Naomi wished her voice wouldn't quaver with her frustration. She grabbed a handful of napkins and began adding them to the place settings in order to keep busy and stop her threatening tears. She was tired of her mother's constant criticism. "It was Susie's idea, and I didn't want to disappoint her. I even invited Levina, Sylvia, and Janie to join us in order to quell any rumors that Sadie Kauffman might feel the need to start about me."

Irma set the casserole dish on the table and pursed her lips. "I know you're not trying to give people the wrong impression, but I know how they think. If you even go for a walk alone with a man, some women assume things they shouldn't about you."

"Why should I care what people think of me?"

"It reflects on this family, Naomi." Irma set the potholders on the counter and then lowered her voice. "How do you think your *dat* will feel if he hears people call you too eager?"

Naomi shook her head. "He would know that I'm not those things, and he would defend me."

Irma touched Naomi's shoulder. "I know you. I know your heart and how you get too attached too soon."

"I'm not attached," Naomi insisted, even though she knew it wasn't the whole truth. "He's *mei freind, Mamm*. What's wrong with being *freinden* with him?"

Irma gave her a sympathetic expression. "I've seen the way you look at him and the way you blush when he's around.

Your feelings for him are written all over your *schee* face, Naomi."

Naomi cupped a hand to her mouth. "They are?"

"*Ya*." Irma touched Naomi's cheek. "I don't want to see you get hurt again. I remember clearly the pain you suffered when you had your heart broken by Luke Troyer and then Timothy Kauffman. I don't want to see you suffer that again, and I don't want you to get a reputation."

"Caleb and I are just *freinden, Mamm*," she repeated, her voice quavering.

Irma raised an eyebrow in disbelief. "Is that what you're trying to convince yourself?"

A lump swelled in Naomi's throat as tears filled her eyes. "It's the truth, *Mamm*."

"He's a widower, Naomi," she said. "He's not ready to give his heart away."

"I know," Naomi whispered. "I've already considered that, and I respect his feelings for his *fraa*."

Her siblings returned to the kitchen with a roar of footsteps, chatter, and giggles, and Naomi breathed a sigh of relief. She longed for her mother's focus to turn to someone other than her.

"Lizzie Anne," Naomi called over the noise. "Would you please grab the glasses from the cabinet?" She glanced at her younger sisters. "You can put the glasses out by the dishes."

Lizzie Anne instructed Amos to go out to the barn and call Elam and their father to come in for supper. She then gave Naomi a concerned expression, but Naomi quickly looked away and turned toward the refrigerator.

Irma grabbed Naomi's arm and pulled her back. "Caleb will

go home to Ohio soon," she whispered in Naomi's ear. "Don't let him take your heart with him. You've been hurt enough."

Naomi sighed with defeat. "Yes, *Mamm*," she said before grabbing the pitcher of ice water and the tub of butter. She took a deep, cleansing breath, pushing away the emotions rioting within her. She knew her mother was right about Caleb's plans to return to Ohio. However, Naomi also couldn't squelch the notion that the feelings she had for Caleb were different from anything she'd ever felt for Luke Troyer or Timothy Kauffman. What she felt for Caleb was deeper, something that touched her soul.

Lizzie Anne sidled up to Naomi. "Are you okay?" she whispered.

Naomi nodded. "*Ya*. I'm *gut*."

Lizzie Anne frowned. "You look upset."

"*Wie geht's?*" Titus's voice boomed as he entered the kitchen. "It smells *appeditlich*."

Naomi forced a smile and touched her sister's arm. "*Danki*," she whispered, "but I'm fine."

Lizzie Anne gave her a look of disbelief.

"It's all ready," Irma said. "*Kinner*, please take your seats."

Naomi delivered the pitcher of water and the butter, placing them near her father's seat, and then sat in her usual place, which was between Lizzie Anne and Elam. As she bowed her head in silent prayer, she asked God to guide her in her confusing feelings for Caleb Schmucker.

❦

"Did you have a *gut* day?" Caleb asked Susie as he sat on the edge of her bed and tucked her in.

"Of course I did, *gegisch*." Susie grinned, hugging her favorite doll to her white nightgown.

He smirked and rubbed her brunette head. Glancing toward the hallway, he wondered how much time he'd have alone with Susie before her cousins came clambering in from the bathroom down the hall. He leaned in close. "Susie, how would you feel about selling our house in Ohio and moving here?"

She gasped, her big, green eyes rounding with excitement. "You mean, like live here forever, *Dat*?"

"*Ya*." He touched the tip of her little nose. "Forever."

She screeched, and he pressed a finger to her lips shushing her.

"Your *onkel* will get very upset if he hears you yell like that," he said.

"Are we going to live here?" she asked, sitting up and gesturing around the room. "Then I can stay in this room with Janie, Nancy, and Linda, and I could go to school with them." Her smile widened. "And maybe I could learn to quilt with *Aenti* Sadie and Naomi. And we could go shopping again with Naomi, and I could play with her sisters. Right, *Dat*?"

He brushed his fingers through her long, brown hair. "*Ya*, maybe so." *And I could spend more time with Naomi as well.*

She leaned forward and wrapped her arms around his neck, hugging him. "*Ich liebe dich, Dat.*"

"I love you too, *boppli*," he whispered before he kissed the top of her head.

Closing his eyes, he sent up a prayer to God, asking Him for help with this decision. While he felt in his heart it was time to move back home, a small part of his mind was apprehensive.

It seemed all the signs were there leading him back home: his family, his friends, the welcoming of the church district members, and the possible opportunity of a job. But was he moving for the right reasons? Would this be a new start or would he be trying to outrun the loneliness that had overtaken his soul when Barbara died? Was he doing this for selfish reasons or did he have his daughter's best interests in mind?

"*Dat?*"

Opening his eyes, he found Susie studying him. "*Ya?*"

Wrinkling her nose, she gave him a confused expression. "Were you sleeping or praying?"

He touched her cheek. "I was praying."

"What were you praying about?"

"I was asking God if He thought we should move back here."

"Oh." She nodded, her expression serious. "And what do you think God's answer was?"

He smiled. "I'm not certain yet, but I'll tell you when He gives me a sign."

"Do you think He'll give me a sign too?"

"Maybe."

She leaned closer and lowered her voice. "You know what Naomi told me?"

"What?"

"She told me that she believes in Christmas miracles," Susie whispered. "Do you believe in them?"

Sighing, he gave her a gentle smile. "Sure I do, Susie."

Muted giggles and loud thumping footsteps echoed down the hallway, announcing the arrival of Susie's cousins. Caleb stood as the girls entered the room and jumped into the beds.

Sadie appeared in the doorway. "It's time to settle down." Crossing the room, she kissed them all on their foreheads.

Caleb wished them each a good night and then followed Sadie down the stairs to the family room.

"Would you like some cocoa?" she asked.

"*Ya. Danki,*" Caleb said.

"Have a seat. I'll be right back." She disappeared into the kitchen.

Caleb sat in a chair in front of the fire, which crackled, popped, and hissed.

Across the room, Robert sat in his favorite chair, reading the paper. Fingering his beard, Caleb wondered what to say to his brother-in-law. Although he'd known Robert since he was a teenager, Caleb never felt much of a connection to him. Not like he did with Timothy and Daniel, anyway. Robert was the least friendly of the Kauffman men. Caleb used to wonder why Robert was so different from his brothers, but he'd finally decided Robert was just stoic. He was more focused on work and running a smooth household and farm than on fun and games.

"I was thinking about going to see that house and workshop that are for sale," Caleb blurted out. "Daniel and Timothy mentioned it was near the furniture store."

Robert peeked at Caleb over the paper. "Really?"

Caleb nodded. "Timothy mentioned that the owner wanted a fair price, and I have some money I've been saving up to rebuild my barn."

Looking intrigued, Robert folded his paper and placed it on the table beside him. "You're considering moving back here, *ya?*"

"I think so." Caleb shifted in the chair. "I mentioned it to Susie, and she's very excited. I think it would be good for her to be with her cousins."

Robert was silent for a moment, fingering his beard and considering Caleb's words. "That makes a lot of sense. It would be *gut* for you and Susie to have a new start, and we would love for you to join our church district."

"*Danki.*" Caleb glanced around the room as memories of his childhood cluttered his mind.

It seemed as if only yesterday he was sitting in this same wing chair and looking at the mantle. The same old, plain cherry clock sat in the center and ticked over the crackle of the fire. The Christmas decorations consisted of a large poinsettia and some greenery, just as when he was a child. For a moment, he expected his father to flop into the armchair across from him, open his Bible, and begin to read aloud while his mother knitted in the love seat next to him.

"Did you have a nice time at the flea market?" Sadie asked, returning from the kitchen holding a tray with three mugs of hot cocoa.

"*Ya*, I did." Caleb lifted a mug from the tray. "*Danki.*"

"*Gern gschehne.*" She handed a mug and napkin to Robert and then sat across from Caleb in their *daed's* favorite chair.

Caleb sipped the mug and felt the whipped cream in his beard. "*Appeditlich.*" He swiped the napkin across his whiskers.

Sadie cradled a mug in her hands. "Susie seemed like she had fun today."

Caleb nodded, sipping more cocoa. "I think she has a *wunderbaar gut* time with her cousin and friends."

"And Naomi." Sadie tapped the side of her mug, a frown turning the corners of her mouth downward.

"*Ya*," he said, ignoring her tone and her expression. "Susie loves spending time with Naomi."

She wagged a finger at him. "You remember what I told you about her."

"Sadie," Robert snapped. "Gossiping is a sin."

Caleb drank from his mug in an effort to suppress the grin threatening to curl his lips. This was one instance in which he appreciated his gruff brother-in-law.

With an indignant frown, Sadie sipped her cocoa.

An awkward silence fell among them as they enjoyed their drinks. Caleb searched for something to say, but found himself only thinking of Naomi and wondering if she'd enjoyed their day together.

After a few sips of cocoa, Robert cleared his throat and glanced at his wife. "Caleb was telling me he wants to go look at the shop that's for sale near my father's store."

"What?" Sadie gasped and grinned. "You're going to consider buying a shop here?"

"Maybe." Caleb held up a hand as if to calm her from across the room. "Don't get your hopes up yet. I'm thinking about moving back, and Timothy and Daniel told me about the shop. Apparently it has a house on the property as well."

Placing her mug on the table beside her, Sadie clapped her hands together. "*Ach*, that's *wunderbaar*. We would love to have you and Susie here."

"Don't get too excited," Caleb repeated. "I discussed it with Susie tonight, and she likes the idea. But I need to do some research and some careful consideration. I have a little bit of money I've been saving to refurbish my barn, but it's only enough for a small down payment. I can't do anything until I get a buyer for my farm. And with today's economy—"

She waved off the thought as she interrupted him. "Your farm would sell easily, Caleb. From what you've told me, you have prime land that an investor would love."

"I'd be glad to take you over to see the shop tomorrow," Robert said. "The owner is Riley Parker, an Englisher who grew up here. He's a *gut* man, and he'll give you a fair price."

Caleb nodded and studied the plain white mug while mulling over the notion of buying a place and setting up business after being gone from Lancaster County for so long. It seemed like such a hasty decision to look at a shop. Would it be prudent to put in an offer? But he wasn't necessarily going to buy it. He was only going to research it and weigh options.

"You know, Caleb," Sadie began, "you don't need to invest in a business quite yet. You could simply take a job working at Wagler's Buggies."

Meeting her probing gaze, Caleb swallowed a sigh, hoping his sister wasn't trying to play matchmaker again. Would she ever listen and respect his decisions? "It's a thought, but I'm not sure I want to be an apprentice anymore. I think I'm ready to open my own shop." His words surprised himself. He hadn't realized he'd wanted to branch out on his own until he said it out loud.

Sadie's eyes widened. "Really?"

Caleb nodded. "I've been working for Jonas since I moved to Middlefield, and as much as I admire him, I think I'm ready to run my own business. As a bonus, he taught me how to make Lancaster-style buggies, in addition to our Ohio ones. So I'd be well prepared to take on business here."

Sadie glanced at Robert, who looked equally shocked.

Robert stood. "I'll take you by there tomorrow. I think I'm going to head up to bed. It's getting late."

Sadie glanced at the clock and popped out of her chair. "Oh my. It's after nine. I best head to bed too." She stepped over to Caleb and glanced at his mug. "Are you finished?"

He shook his head. "No, I've been savoring it." He smiled up at her. "I think I'll sit here for a few minutes and enjoy the fire. I'll clean up after myself."

She patted his shoulder. "*Gut nacht, bruder.* I do hope you decide to stay."

"*Danki.*" He frowned. "Don't start any rumors about my moving here, Sadie. Right now I'm trying to figure out God's plan for Susie and me."

She gasped. "I'll do no such thing, Caleb. I'll keep it to myself."

He raised an eyebrow with suspicion.

She made a motion as if to zip her lips and then headed into the kitchen.

Sighing, Caleb leaned his head back on the chair and closed his eyes. Opening his heart to God, Caleb silently asked Him to reveal the right path for him and his precious daughter.

CHAPTER 10

Caleb steered the horse toward the For Sale sign sitting at the edge of the property. Since Robert had to tend to business at the farm, Caleb had borrowed the horse and buggy and ventured out to find the place on his own.

Guiding the horse into a rock driveway, Caleb spotted a large cinderblock building containing three bay doors and an office off to the right. He stopped the horse by the office door, and his boots crunched across the snow as he walked around to the front of the building. Caleb climbed the stairs, and the door opened with a loud squeak, revealing a stocky middle-aged English man with dark hair and eyes.

"Good morning," the man said. "May I help you?"

"Yes," Caleb said. "My name is Caleb Schmucker, and I wanted to speak with the owner regarding the price of this property."

"I'm the owner, and it's nice to meet you." The man shook Caleb's hand. "I'm Riley Parker. Please come in." He gestured for Caleb to enter the shop. "I'm glad you came by. Do you live around here?"

"No. I'm visiting from Ohio. My sister lives in Bird-in-Hand." Caleb glanced around the office, which was a small room that led to the large work bays. "My daughter and I are here for the holidays, and I'm considering moving back."

"Oh." Riley rubbed the stubble on his chin. "You're from around here originally?"

Caleb nodded. "That's right. I moved to Ohio about ten years ago after I got married. My wife passed away two years ago, and I don't have any family there, except for a few of her cousins."

Riley frowned. "I'm sorry for your loss."

"*Danki.*" Caleb smiled. "I'm thinking that I want to come back here so that my daughter has some family around her while she grows up."

"Yes, family is important." Riley leaned on the counter behind him. "I know quite a few Amish families around here. Who is your sister?"

"Sadie Kauffman." He jammed his thumb toward the door as if in the direction of the road. "Her husband's family owns the furniture store a few blocks down."

"Oh!" Riley nodded. "I know Eli Kauffman quite well. Nice family."

"Yes." Caleb stepped over to the door and looked toward the bays, imagining his toolboxes and supplies lining the walls while he built buggies. He could see himself coming here every day and working to make a living. "This is a nice place you have here. Have you owned it long?"

"Oh yeah." Riley limped toward the bays and motioned for Caleb to follow. "This land has been in my family for years. My father built this shop about fifty years ago, and I added on twenty years ago. I ran a towing company and did some minor car repairs on the side." He patted his thigh.

"I've got a bum leg, so I can't work much anymore. My kids have all married and moved away, and my wife and I decided it was time to retire and move to Florida. But we need to unload this place before I can buy my condo."

Riley gestured toward the row of toolboxes and work-benches. "I'll have all of this cleared out soon. My youngest son is supposed to come and get the tools at some point. I don't want to take any of them to Florida." He smiled. "Well, just a little box with the basics for the honey-do lists my wife likes to make to keep me off the sofa."

Caleb walked the length of the shop, imagining how he would set it up if it were his. The building was bigger than the shop he worked in back in Ohio. "This is quite spacious."

Riley moved the curtain and pointed toward a brick home behind the shop. "The house is out back if you'd like to see that too."

"*Danki.*" Caleb followed Riley out a side door and down the driveway.

"We have a barn out back too," Riley said, pointing toward a small fenced pasture. "It's not big, but it's functional if you have a few animals."

"How many acres are here?"

"Six," Riley said as they approached the brick ranch house. "The house has three bedrooms and two bathrooms. The rooms are fairly big. We raised four boys without any problems. Would you like to come in? My wife is at the market right now, but I would be happy to show you around."

"That would be great," Caleb said.

While Riley led him around the house, Caleb imagined making a home for him and Susie. The bedrooms were a good size, and the woodwork on the trim in the little house was also nice. The house was nothing fancy, but Caleb didn't need fancy.

Before he could move in, he would have to have the electricity removed from the house in order to keep with his Amish traditions. He would also need to convert to gas appliances, but that wouldn't be a problem.

Caleb glanced around the kitchen, trying to imagine his table and chairs in the center of the room. His heart warmed at the idea of being home in Lancaster County, celebrating holidays and milestones with his sister and her family, worshipping with her church district and his old friends. He would also make new friends, and he would possibly get to know a very special friend better: Naomi King.

His last thought caused him to smile to himself. He would definitely enjoy spending time with Naomi, as would Susie.

Caleb turned to Riley, standing in the doorway to the family room. "May I see the barn?"

"Sure." Riley led him out through the small one-car garage toward the pasture.

Stepping into the barn, an overwhelming calmness enveloped Caleb. He glanced around at the horse stalls, and he knew—this was the house. This was meant to be for him and Susie.

This was the sign from God he'd been waiting for.

Smiling, Caleb faced Riley in the doorway. "What's your final price, Mr. Parker?"

❧

Later that afternoon, Caleb steered the buggy into Sadie's

driveway. After putting up the horse and buggy, he grabbed his armload of bags from his shopping trip and headed up the back steps. Entering the kitchen, he found Susie sitting at the table eating cookies with her cousins.

"*Dat*!" she called when she spotted him. "Look at the cookies we made at Naomi's today." She held up a plate with assorted Christmas cookies. "Levina and Sylvia invited us over after school. We had fun."

"Oh my." Dropping his bags on the floor, Caleb swiped a chocolate chip cookie from the plate and took a bite. "*Appeditlich*!" He finished the cookie in two big bites and then hung his coat on the peg by the door before kicking off his boots.

Susie leaned over and examined the pile of bags. "What's in there?"

He picked up the bags and held them close to his body. "Nothing for you to be concerned about." He backed out of the kitchen. "Enjoy your cookies, girls."

Caleb crossed the family room and into his parents' former apartment where he'd been staying. He walked through the small sitting room to the bedroom and dropped the bags onto the bed. He then opened the closet to make room for the gifts. He was placing the bag from the bookstore onto the top shelf of the closet when a knock sounded on the door frame.

Sadie stepped into the room with a curious expression. "How was your visit to the Parker place?"

"*Gut*." Caleb lowered himself onto the bed, and it creaked beneath his weight.

"Oh?" She raised her eyebrows with curiosity.

He crossed his arms over his wide chest. "I made an offer."

She gasped and clasped her hands together. "My *bruder* is moving back home!"

He nodded and smiled. "I think so."

"*Ach*! This is *wunderbaar gut*!" Sadie gestured widely with an equally wide grin. "Our *kinner* will go to school together. We'll worship together and also celebrate birthdays and holidays together! This is a dream come true. I'm so *froh*!"

"Don't get too excited just yet," he said, standing. "I have to try to sell my farm and then it will take some time to get my business going here. I'm hoping I can make a smooth transition from Jonas's shop to my own."

"Wait." She held a hand up. "You shouldn't open your own business just yet. You should work for Hezekiah Wagler until you have enough money to open your own business. That way you could—"

"Sadie," he began, his voice firm. "Stop trying to set me up with Irene Wagler."

"What are you implying, Caleb?" Her surprised expression was forced. "I'm not trying to set you up. I'm just looking after your finances."

He glowered at his older sister. "I can look after my own finances just fine, *danki*. I'm a grown man. I also will decide if and when I'm ready to court women."

She frowned, looking hurt by his words. "Caleb, I only have your best interests in mind. I want you to make the right decisions for you and Susie."

"I can make my own decisions, *danki*." He spotted Susie crossing the sitting room and heading for the door, and he bit back the angry words that were bubbling forth from his throat.

"*Dat!*" Susie bounded into the room. "Where did you go today? I thought you'd be home sooner."

"I told you," he said, forcing a smile for his daughter's sake. "I ran a few errands."

"Errands?" Sadie asked.

He nodded at Sadie and then glanced at Susie. "I just had a few things I needed to pick up at the store while I was out."

Susie looked curious. "Oh. Did you have a *gut* day?"

"I did," Caleb said. "Did you have a *gut* day?"

Susie nodded. "I had lots of fun with my cousins."

"I'm going to go start supper." Sadie stepped toward the door. "Did you tell Susie the exciting news?"

Susie's eyes rounded. "What news?"

"It looks like we're going to move here," he said slowly. "I talked to a man about a house today."

"Yeah!" Susie wrapped her arms around Caleb's neck, and he hugged her.

Caleb glanced toward the doorway. Seeing that Sadie was gone, he breathed a sigh of relief. While he loved his sister, he grew weary of her constant interference. He hoped that moving closer to her wouldn't be a mistake. However, in his heart, he knew this was the best plan for him and Susie. Besides, he could get to know Naomi better and see if his growing feelings for her would turn into something more permanent.

And that was when Caleb realized the truth: he was planning this move for himself as much as for Susie. God wanted him to break free of the loneliness that had hung over him like a black cloud since Barbara's death. Caleb believed he was entitled to find happiness again even though Barbara was gone.

CHAPTER 11

I can't believe Christmas Eve is tomorrow," Naomi said as she walked through the indoor flea market on Friday.

"I know." Lilly stopped and glanced at the candy concession stand. "I should get some candy for Hannah's *kinner*." She smiled at the clerk and began rattling off a list of candy.

Lizzie Anne sidled up to Naomi and tapped her shoulder. "Are you okay?" she whispered. "You've been sort of quiet since Wednesday. Is everything all right?"

Naomi held back a sigh. Her younger sister was quite intuitive. Naomi had been quiet since her discussion with her mother Wednesday night, after her shopping excursion with Caleb and the girls. And Naomi's reticence was caused by the conflicting thoughts swirling through her head. Her mother had warned her not to allow Caleb to return to Ohio with her heart. While Naomi knew that the advice was sound, she feared that Caleb Schmucker already had possession of it.

Naomi tried to smile, but her lips formed a grimace. "I have some things on my mind."

"Is something wrong?" Lizzie Anne asked, her brown eyes full of worry.

"No," Naomi said, glancing toward the counter, where

Lilly stood talking to the candy clerk. "Everything is fine. I just have a lot to get done. I still have to make a batch of butterscotch cookies for *Dat* and then get all of the gifts together for the little ones."

Lizzie Anne tilted her chin in question. "Are you certain that's it?"

"*Ya*." Naomi pulled her list from the pocket of her apron. "I need to pick up a few gifts for *Mamm*. She wants me to get some little gifts in case we go visiting tomorrow."

"For the Kauffmans, *ya*?"

Naomi's eyes snapped to her sister's face. "The Kauffmans?"

"*Ya*. We were invited to Sadie's tomorrow night for the Kauffman Christmas Eve get-together," Lizzie Anne said with a smile. "I have to pick up something special for Lindsay," she said, referring to Rebecca Kauffman's niece who lived with her. "You know she's my best *freind*."

Nodding, Naomi had wondered when she would see Caleb again. Although the thought of seeing him again sent her stomach into a knot, she also couldn't wait. She'd enjoyed the time spent baking and laughing with Susie and her sisters yesterday afternoon. She felt her attachment to the girl growing, but she also knew the attachment wasn't limited to just the girl. She had deep, growing feelings for Susie's father, and it both scared and excited her at the same time. And this feeling was nothing compared to what she'd believed she felt for Luke Troyer and Timothy Kauffman once. This attachment was more meaningful. The risk of heartbreak was high, but for some inexplicable reason, Naomi felt a willingness to take the risk.

"Naomi?" a voice asked.

Naomi turned and found Lilly studying her.

"You okay?" her friend asked.

"Funny," Lizzie Anne began with a grin. "I just asked her the same question."

Naomi blew out a defeated sigh. "I feel like I'm on trial here."

Lilly took Naomi's arm and pulled her through the knot of shoppers. "Let's go get some fudge and talk."

"Fine." Naomi gave in with a grimace. Getting fudge would bring back memories of her shopping day with Caleb. How ironic.

After ordering the chocolate, they sat at a small table. Naomi felt her sister's and her friend's eyes studying her as she broke off a piece of milk chocolate fudge.

"What's going on?" Lilly asked between bites of her dark chocolate fudge. "You're very distracted and quiet."

"That's what I said," Lizzie Anne said while wiping a piece of milk chocolate off her sleeve and balancing her slab of remaining fudge in her other hand.

"I have a lot on my mind," Naomi said with a shrug.

"Such as?" Lilly prodded.

Naomi knew neither of them would back down until she spilled her heart to them. It was time to confess her feelings, and she wasn't certain she could put them into coherent words.

"On Wednesday, I went shopping with Caleb Schmucker, Susie, Janie Kauffman, and my younger sisters," Naomi said, keeping her eyes on her block of fudge. "In fact, we came here, so Susie could do some Christmas shopping for little gifts for her cousins and new friends."

"What?" Lilly's voice nearly squeaked with shock. "Why didn't you tell me this yesterday?"

"I didn't think to tell you." Naomi felt wretched for telling a fib, but she continued, despite Lilly's hurt expression. "That night, my *mamm* gave me a lecture on not giving my heart to Caleb because he's a widower and also because he's going to go back to Ohio. She said I'm just setting myself up to get hurt."

"Why would *Mamm* say that?" Lizzie Anne asked while wiping more stray crumbs off her sleeve. "Why does *Mamm* think you like Caleb?"

"I don't know." Naomi's cheeks heated. She wasn't very good at lying.

"Oh," Lizzie Anne said with a wide smile. "You do like Caleb."

"*Mamms* have a way of knowing these things," Lilly said, patting Lizzie Anne's arm. "Sometimes they know before we do. It's their job." She then turned her gaze to Naomi. "How did shopping go? Did you have a *gut* time?"

Naomi nodded. "We had a *wunderbaar* time. He's so easy to talk to, and he's so very sweet and thoughtful." She frowned and shook her head. "I'm doomed. I never should've gone out with him."

"Why do you say that?" Lizzie Anne asked. She bit into the fudge, and the crumbs were finally under control. "It sounds like you're *gut freinden*. Why can't you be *freinden* with him? Susie obviously likes you. I've seen how she talks to you and follows you around."

"It's more complicated than that," Naomi said with a gentle smile. She ate more fudge and wished she could turn off her feelings for Caleb. But did she really want to turn them off? When she was with him, she felt a true happiness that she'd never felt before.

"You're not going to listen to your *mamm* are you?" Lilly asked before popping a final piece of fudge into her mouth.

"I don't know." Naomi shrugged. "I don't know what to do. My *mamm* is right about him leaving. He's going to go back to Ohio, and where will that leave me? I'll be right back where I was when Timothy and I broke up—alone and nursing a broken heart."

"Maybe not," Lizzie Anne said. "Maybe he'll want to court you, and he and Susie can move here." She shrugged. "He may like you too, and he may want to be back by his family since Susie's *mamm* is gone." She looked between Lilly and Naomi. "It's a possibility, right?"

Lilly nodded. "You could be right."

Naomi shook her head. "That would be a big move for him."

"Or you could move to Ohio," Lizzie Anne said. "I would hate to see you go, but we could visit."

Naomi shook her head. "I don't know if I could leave *Mamm*, *Dat*, and all of you."

"It would be difficult, but my cousin did it," Lilly said. "She misses her family, but she keeps in touch with letters and occasional phone calls."

"Lilly is right." Lizzie Anne wiped her mouth. "If it feels right for you to go with him to Ohio, then you should think about it. You need to follow your heart, Naomi. That's what you used to say."

"I was wrong," Naomi whispered, thinking back on her failed relationships.

"No, you were never wrong about following your heart," Lilly chimed in with a knowing smile. "You simply did it at the wrong time. Don't judge your future by your past. Things happen in God's time."

"*Ya!*" Lizzie Anne snapped her fingers. "It's like the verse *Dat* read last night during devotions. Remember? I think it went something like: 'I wait for the Lord, my soul waits, and in his word I put my hope.'"

Lilly grinned at Lizzie Anne. "You are one smart *maedel*."

Lizzie Anne smoothed the tie of her prayer covering. "Sometimes I have a *gut* thought or two."

Naomi smiled while finishing her fudge.

"It's like what you told me the other day," Lilly said. "You said that in the past you were too eager and you didn't wait for God's time for love. Maybe now it's God's time."

Naomi nodded slowly while considering the words. "Maybe it is." *I hope you're right, Lilly.*

Lilly wiped her hands and stood. "Let's shop, *ya?*"

Naomi tossed her dirty napkins in the trash can. "I have a store I want to go into."

Lizzie Anne chatted about the weather report and threat of more snow as they weaved through the crowd toward the antique store.

"What are we doing here?" Lizzie Anne asked as they stepped through the doorway.

"I'll be fast," Naomi said and then rushed toward the tool section, holding her breath and hoping that the antique drill was still there. She picked up the contraption and smiled.

After paying for it, she hurried over to Lizzie Anne and Lilly, who were in a deep discussion about a desk and whether or not it was an antique or just an overpriced piece of furniture.

"Did you get what you needed?" Lilly asked as they headed back out into the flea market crowd.

"*Ya*," Naomi hugged the bag to her cloak. "I'm all set. I just need to go to the toy store and find some little things for the *kinner*."

"What's in the bag?" Lizzie Anne reached for the bag.

Naomi swatted her hand away. "Nothing."

Her sister's eyes widened with curiosity. "*Ach*, then it must be *gut*. Is it for Caleb?"

Naomi nodded.

"What is it?" Lilly asked, looking intrigued.

"It's something he told me he wanted but would never buy himself," Naomi said, loosening her grip on the bag.

"What is it?" Lizzie Anne asked again. "Just tell us. We'll keep it a secret, right, Lilly?"

Lilly nodded. "You have my word."

Naomi moved out of the crowd and stood outside the toy store. She pulled out the drill, and Lilly and Lizzie Anne stared at the tool as if it were from another world.

"What is it?" Lizzie Anne asked.

"It looks sort of like a drill my *grossdaddi* had in his barn," Lilly said.

"That's exactly what it is, Lilly," Naomi said. "Caleb collects antique tools, and he uses them too."

"Wow," Lizzie Anne said, touching the handle. "He'll love it."

Naomi smiled. "I hope so."

CHAPTER 12

Caleb was reading his Bible when a knock sounded on his bedroom door later that evening. He opened the door and found Susie glowering. "*Wie geht's?*"

"Irene is here." She spat out the words. "I don't think I like her."

He raised an eyebrow. "Susan. What's gotten into you?"

"She doesn't even say hello to me," Susie said, her frown deepening. "She looked at me and said, 'Where's your *dat*?' It's like I don't exist."

Caleb touched her prayer covering. "I'm certain she didn't mean it. Remember your manners."

"Why?" Susie asked as they headed through the sitting room. "She doesn't remember hers, so why should I remember mine?"

He suppressed a smile. "You must always be respectful of adults, even when it seems as if they don't have any manners. Maybe she will learn by your example."

"Yes, *Dat*." She stopped at the doorway leading to the large family room. "But I'm certain she doesn't like me," she whispered, her pretty face twisted with a deep scowl.

He touched her nose. "Anyone who doesn't like you is misled, *mei liewe.*"

She scrunched her nose, and he laughed. Taking her hand, he steered her to the kitchen where Irene sat talking with Sadie. Sadie's younger children were seated at the table coloring on construction paper.

"*Wie geht's?*" Caleb said.

"Oh, Caleb," Sadie said, popping up from her chair. "I'll let you two chat." She shooed her children into the family room and then looked at Susie. "You come too, Susie. Let your *dat* and Irene chat."

Susie frowned up at Sadie. "I'm staying with my *dat.*"

Sadie lifted a finger in preparation to scold her.

"She's fine," Caleb said, his voice booming a little louder than he'd intended.

"Oh," Sadie said, looking surprised. She disappeared into the family room.

"*Wie geht's?*" Caleb repeated, sinking into a chair across the table from Irene.

"I'm *gut*. How are you?" Irene smiled sweetly at Caleb and then glanced past him, her smile fading.

Caleb turned to find Susie leaning in the doorway, looking unhappy. "Join us, Susie." He motioned for her to come to the table, but she shook her head. He could feel her uneasiness from across the room, and his heart ached for his usually happy-go-lucky daughter.

He turned back to Irene, and her sugary sweet smile returned. "What brings you out this way?" he inquired, hoping to ease the tension.

"I was going to ask you what you were planning for

supper," she said, leaning across the table just slightly as if to share a secret. "Do you like Hamburg goulash?"

"*Ach,*" he said, fingering his beard. "I'd have to count that as one of my most favorite meals."

"*Gut!*" She grinned. "Why don't you grab your coat, and we'll head out to my parents' house. I made a special dessert too."

"Sounds *appeditlich.*" He turned to Susie, who was still in the doorway, twisting one of the ties from her prayer covering in her little finger. "Grab your cloak, Susie. We're going to dinner at Irene's."

"Oh," Irene said quickly. She leaned toward him and lowered her voice. "I thought maybe Susie could stay here with Sadie so that you and my *dat* could talk about the shop."

"See, *Dat,*" Susie exclaimed, stomping into the room. "She doesn't like me!"

"Susan." Caleb stood. He gestured for her to calm down while working to keep his voice composed. "We just talked about this. Remember your manners." He turned to Irene. "I'd rather not have dinner without my *dochder.*"

Irene bristled. "Oh. I thought you might like to discuss the buggy business without the interruption of a *kind.*"

"I don't see my *dochder* as an interruption." He walked over to Susie and placed a hand on her shoulder.

Irene looked stunned. "But don't you want to discuss working at my *daed's* shop?"

Caleb shook his head. "If she's not welcome, then I'll politely turn down your supper invitation." He glanced down at Susie, and she smiled. Her eyes were so full of love that his heart felt as if it would melt.

Popping up, Irene crossed to the door and snatched her cloak from the peg on the wall. "I suppose I'll see you later." Scowling, she pulled on her cloak. "Please tell Sadie I said *gut nacht*."

"I will," Caleb said, gently squeezing Susie's shoulder.

Irene rushed through the door, which slammed behind her.

"*Dat!*" Susie beamed up at him. "You didn't want to go without me?"

He shook his head. "How could I go without you? You're *mei liewe*. We're in this together, remember?"

She wrapped her arms around his waist and hugged him. "*Ich liebe dich.*"

"I love you too," he said. "But you must remember not to talk back to adults, Susie. You can get your point across without being rude."

She grinned up at him. "Like you did."

He chuckled and rubbed her shoulder. "*Ya*, I guess I did."

She headed for the door. "I'm going to go tell Janie!"

"Susie!" He hoped to stop her from telling the family about his conversation with Irene, but she was gone. He heard her shoes clunking up the stairs to the bedrooms.

Stepping over to the window, Caleb glanced out at the sky, seeing snowflakes floating down to the porch railing and dotting the rock driveway.

"Did I hear a door slam?" Sadie asked behind him.

"*Ya*," he said, facing her quizzical stare. "Irene left."

Sadie stepped through the doorway. "Didn't she invite you for supper?"

He nodded. "She did."

"And what happened?" Her eyes searched his face.

"I declined her invitation."

"Why would you do that?" She stepped toward him. "I don't understand. Irene is young and attractive, and her father has a successful carriage shop. You don't need to invest in a new business." She gestured with her hands. "You could simply work for him, and you and Irene could get to know each other better."

He frowned, running his hand through his hair. Would his sister ever stop her interfering? "I'm going for a walk." He gripped the doorknob and wrenched the back door open with a squeak.

"Caleb?" Sadie called after him.

Stepping out onto the porch, the cold, moist air seeped through his shirt and into his skin. He took a deep, cleansing breath and walked over to the railing. Closing his eyes, he let the cool snowflakes kiss his warm cheeks while breathing out the frustration boiling in his soul.

He knew that allowing his sister's interference to upset him wouldn't help the situation. He remembered clearly how she tried to run his life when he lived with his parents. She was interested in all of Caleb's comings and goings, suggesting how he should spend his social life and even giving her unsolicited opinions of his friends. While he loved his sister, she was a hopeless meddler.

Opening his eyes, he stared up at the sky, wondering how he would handle her when he moved back. How could he keep the lines of communication open with his sister without losing his temper?

He glanced toward the driveway, and his thoughts turned

to Irene. He'd hoped that Susie was wrong when she'd proclaimed Irene's dislike for her. However, Irene's facial expressions and her blatant disregard for Susie's feelings were apparent. He'd never understand how someone could disregard a child the way that Irene did. Even if Caleb had wanted to discuss business with Hezekiah Wagler, he would've done it in front of Susie. She was old enough to be quiet while the adults were having a serious conversation.

He turned back toward the pasture. If he cut across the pasture and continued about a half mile, he would wind up on Naomi's road. He wondered if she was home. And if so, would she want to visit with him? He hadn't seen her since Wednesday, and he missed her. He wondered if she missed him too.

Caleb snickered to himself. He sounded like a lovesick teenage boy.

"*Dat?*" Susie's voice sounded behind him.

He faced her and swallowed a shiver. "Susie?" he asked with a smile.

She jammed a hand on her little hip. "You know you're going to catch a cold, *ya?*"

He nodded. "*Ya.* I know."

She smiled. "Janie says you're a *wunderbaar gut dat* for what you said to Irene Wagler."

He grinned. "I'm *froh* she approves."

"I like Naomi more than I like Irene," she said.

"*Ya*, I know," he said. "I can't blame you."

"Are you going to come inside or do I need to get you your coat?" She frowned, and her face reminded him of Barbara's when she disapproved of something Caleb had done.

"I'll be in shortly," he said, rubbing his arms.

She gave him a confused expression, shrugged, and closed the door.

He looked back up at the sky and prayed for strength and help for dealing with both his sister and the uncertainties of the upcoming move from Ohio to Pennsylvania.

CHAPTER 13

It's a regular blizzard out here," Naomi commented, climbing from Lilly's buggy. She helped her siblings out of the back and then grabbed her bag of gifts. "Lizzie Anne and Levina, grab those platters of cookies and carry them in please. Sylvia, please take the bag with the gifts for the *kinner.*"

"I can't believe the snow." Lilly tented her hand over her eyes to block the raging flurries. "I don't know how we're going to find our way home."

Stepping on the sidewalk, Sylvia slipped and then righted herself. "Maybe we'll have to stay the night."

Naomi chuckled. "I don't think Sadie has enough room for all of us."

Naomi, her younger siblings, and Lilly made their way up the steps to the porch. A buggy bounced up the drive, leaving tracks revealing its path, and Naomi spotted her parents and Elam emerging from the buggy into the snow. Elam stowed her parents' horse and Lilly's horse, and her parents began their trek through the blowing snow to the stairs. Naomi waited for her parents while Lilly and Naomi's siblings disappeared into the house, carrying the food and gifts.

"Naomi, you should go inside," Titus said on his way up the stairs. Moving past her, he held the door open. "Go on. You'll catch a cold."

"*Danki, Dat,*" Naomi said with a smile. She gestured for her mother to go in first. "After you, *Mamm.*"

"*Danki.*" Her mother smiled as she stepped into the foyer. "I assume the *kinner* brought in the food and gifts?"

"*Ya.*" Naomi followed Irma into the family room and then helped her remove her cloak.

They hung their cloaks on the pegs on the wall, jamming them on top of the pile and then stepped into the family room, clogged with people talking and laughing. Irma disappeared into the crowd, shaking hands and greeting friends while smiling.

Naomi scanned the group, her stomach fluttering as she searched for one certain face: Caleb's.

"Naomi!" A little voice yelled as a hand pulled on the skirt of her frock. "*Frehlicher Grischtdaag!*"

Naomi glanced down into Susie's smiling face. "Oh, Susie." She hugged the little girl. "*Frehlicher Grischtdaag* to you too! I have something for you." She perused the crowd, looking for one of her siblings and her bag of gifts.

"I have something for you!" Taking her hand, Susie yanked Naomi toward the far side of the family room. "I'll have to find my gifts."

They crossed the family room, and Naomi glanced through another doorway into a smaller sitting room, where she spotted Caleb standing with Timothy Kauffman and Hezekiah Wagler. The three men were talking and laughing while holding mugs, which she assumed were full of Robert's famous hot cider.

Susie dug through a large shopping bag and then pulled out a small doll. "This is for you."

Naomi held the doll up and examined it. The tiny, cloth doll wore a blue dress, black apron, and black winter bonnet, and held a little sign that said "Friends." Tears filled Naomi's eyes as she looked at Susie. "It's *schee*."

Susie beamed. "I got it for you because you're *mei freind*."

"It's perfect." Leaning down, Naomi engulfed Susie into a hug and squeezed her tight.

When she stood, she felt someone's stare focused on her. Glancing over, she spotted Caleb watching her. He nodded and smiled, and she returned the gesture before turning back to Susie.

"Now, I hope you don't think this is *gegisch*, but I got you something too." Naomi put the doll into the pocket of her apron and then reached into her bag and pulled out the quilt she'd shown Susie during the quilting bee. "This is for you."

"For me?" Susie gasped as she hugged the quilt to her chest. "I love this so much! I will sleep with it on my bed every night. *Danki*, Naomi."

"*Gern gschehne*. That's not all." Naomi then pulled out a flat box. "This was my favorite game when I was your age." She held her breath, hoping Susie would like it.

"Scrabble!" Susie's green eyes rounded with excitement as she draped the quilt over her arm. "Oh, Naomi! *Danki*!" She hugged Naomi again, and Naomi chuckled. "Will you play with me?"

"Of course," Naomi said. "I think it's too crowded to play here now, but I promise we'll get in at least one game before you and your *dat* head back to Ohio."

Susie examined the box. "Then you'll play more when we get back, right?"

"*Ya*," Naomi said. "If you bring it each time you visit, we'll play it. I don't think my game at home has all of the pieces anymore." She gripped the handles of her shopping bag, wondering when to give Caleb his special gift.

"Not when we visit." Susie looked up. "I mean when we move here."

Naomi gasped. "What did you say?"

Susie grinned. "We're moving here. My *dat* said he found a house."

Stunned, Naomi was speechless. She looked toward Caleb and found him nodding while listening to Hezekiah. Her heart filled with warmth and hope of a possible future with Caleb and Susie. Maybe they could be a family? Was this what Lizzie Anne had been talking about with her verse about waiting for the Lord and putting hope in Him? Was it God's time for her like Lilly had said?

She glanced back at Susie. "Are you certain?"

Susie nodded. "*Ya*. I heard my *Aenti* Sadie say something about *Dat* working for Irene's *daed*." She frowned. "I hope that isn't true. Irene doesn't like me. She doesn't smile at me. She invited my *dat* over for supper and said I wasn't invited. She's not very nice."

Naomi swallowed a groan as her hopes evaporated. Caleb's plans included Irene, not Naomi. "Oh," she said, her voice barely a whisper over the conversations floating around them.

"Irene is always smiling around my *dat*," Susie continued, looking disgusted. "She always wants to be with him alone. She acts nice around him, but she's not really nice at all."

Speechless, Naomi listened as her frown deepened.

"She acts like I don't exist," Susie said, gripping the box and the quilt in her arms. "She doesn't even want me in the room with her and my *dat*." She glowered. "My *dat* says I have to respect adults and use my manners, but I don't want to use my manners around her." Her expression softened. "But you're always so nice to me. You're *mei freind* and I could never be friends with Irene. I know it's not Christian to say that, but it's the truth."

Naomi nodded again. She couldn't form the words to express the emotions that were weighing down on her shoulders. She felt her spirit wilting, like a thirsty flower in desperate need of water.

"I want my *dat* to be with you, not Irene. I don't understand why he even talks to her. Irene would never bake with me or quilt with me. She would never even play a game with me." Susie placed the flat box and the quilt on the bench next to her and began to open the box. "Can we play now?"

"I don't think that would be a *gut* idea," Naomi said, hoping her anxiety didn't show on her face. "There are too many people here, and I'm afraid the pieces will get lost."

"Oh." Susie looked disappointed. "I can't wait to play. Maybe we can go up to my room." She nodded toward the sitting room behind them. "Or maybe my *dat's* room on the coffee table? We could spread the game out and play."

Naomi glanced toward the sitting room and spotted Irene standing next to Caleb while her father chatted. Caleb and Timothy both laughed at something Hezekiah said, and Naomi's heart sank. She'd been so wrong about Caleb. And now that he was going to move here, she'd have to see him and endure the sting of her heartache just as she had to endure seeing Luke Troyer and Timothy Kauffman. She felt herself falling into a pit of despair, as if her heart were being smashed into a million pieces right before her eyes.

Her stomach twisted, and she glanced at Susie. "I'm not feeling well. I think I need to go get something to drink."

Susie hoisted her game and quilt. "I'll come with you. Let me just run these upstairs." She trotted through the knot of people toward the stairs.

Naomi moved past familiar faces, nodding and shaking hands on her way to the kitchen. She reached the kitchen doorway and stopped when she spotted Sadie speaking to one of her quilting friends.

"Oh, *ya*," Sadie said. "Caleb and Susie love it here. In fact, he put a bid in on Riley Parker's place. You know, the one by the furniture store."

"Oh, right," her friend said. "The one with the little workshop."

"That's right," Sadie said. "But I told him not to open a shop. He can work for Hezekiah Wagler." She smiled. "Caleb and Irene would make such a *wunderbaar* couple. As we all know, Susie needs the guidance that only a *mamm* can supply."

Naomi's stomach clenched and bile rose in her throat. She had to make a quick getaway before she became physically ill. She spun on her heel and rushed through the crowd toward the front door.

"Naomi!" a voice called.

Naomi forged ahead, ignoring the voice.

"Wait!" A hand grabbed Naomi's arm and pulled her off balance, causing her to stumble.

Naomi turned to find Lilly studying her.

"Where are you going?" Lilly asked.

"I don't feel well," Naomi said. And it wasn't a lie. She felt as if she were going to be sick, and she couldn't allow herself to be sick in public, especially in Sadie Kauffman's home.

Susie rushed over to them. "Naomi! Let's go get a drink." She took Naomi's hand.

"I'm sorry, Susie." Naomi touched the girl's cheek. "I'm not feeling well, so I'm going to head home. *Danki* for the gift."

Susie frowned. "But I thought we were going to spend time together."

"Not tonight." Naomi glanced down at the bag containing Caleb's gift. She held it out. "Would you please make sure your *dat* gets this? Tell him that it's from me, *ya?*"

Looking disappointed, Susie took the bag. "Okay."

"Good night." Naomi leaned down and kissed Susie's cheek. She then hugged Lilly. "I'll talk to you soon."

Lilly shook her head. "You shouldn't go out into that blizzard alone. Let me find Elam for you."

Naomi touched Lilly's shoulder. "I'll be fine. When I was seventeen, I left the house alone to get some medicine for Amos because he was really sick. On the way back from the store, my buggy broke down in the snow not too far from here. I had to leave the horse and buggy and walk home in a blizzard. I found my way, and everything was okay." She pulled on her cloak. "I know I can do this."

Before Lilly could respond, Naomi slipped out the door. She almost slipped twice on her way down the porch steps. The snow swirled around her, blinding her vision and soaking her cloak as she slowly moved down the driveway.

I can do this. I have to do it. I can't fall to pieces in front of Caleb, the Kauffmans, and the rest of the community.

Stopping at the pasture fence, she considered which route to take home. Although she couldn't see much beyond the fence, she knew that if she crossed the pasture, she could then cut through two farms and find her way to her road. It looked similar to the route she'd taken when her buggy had broken down years ago.

Heaving a deep breath, she began to trudge through the snow, shivering and gritting her teeth. The further she moved, the less she could see in front of her.

What was I thinking? This is a bad idea.

Naomi glanced back in the direction of what she thought was Sadie's home, but she couldn't see the outline of the house, not even the pitch of the roof.

She turned completely around in a circle and couldn't see anything except for snow. Her teeth chattered, and her eyes filled with frustrated tears.

I'm lost.

She looked straight up toward the white sky, and large, moist flakes blinded her.

Naomi gazed in the direction that she thought was the road and then trudged ahead two steps. She then moved forward, and her foot landed in a hole, causing her ankle to twist in an awkward direction. Screaming out loud, she wobbled, fell, and rolled down a hill. The sting of pain shot like lightning from her ankle up her leg.

She tried to lift her leg, but she couldn't move it. Taking a deep breath, she attempted to sit up, but the sting in her ankle forced her to stop.

Sobbing, Naomi rolled to her side and prayed that someone would come and find her while the bitter cold air closed
in around her, prickling her skin like thousands of tiny icicles.

CHAPTER 14

Caleb smiled and nodded, wondering if Hezekiah Wagler would ever take a breath. Irene stood across from her father and chimed in frequently, adding details to the man's endless stories about his business, mechanical techniques, old friends, and family memories. Caleb was surprised Irene was even speaking to him, but she acted as if nothing had happened the previous day.

Glancing toward the door, Caleb noticed that the crowd in the main family room was dissipating. Timothy had left the conversation to join his fiancée and her family quite a while ago. Caleb had hoped Timothy would return and rescue him from the Waglers, but Timothy was a smart man and had stayed away. Caleb wondered how long it had been since his best friend had abandoned him. Had it been more than an hour? Had Caleb missed the entire Christmas party?

Susie, Janie, Nancy, and Linda scampered into the sitting room and gathered around the coffee table where Susie opened a Scrabble board game box. Taking out the contents of the box, the girls giggled while setting up their letters. Caleb swallowed a sigh of relief. This was his chance to break away and try to find Naomi. He couldn't wait to give her the special Christmas gift he'd picked up for her.

"It's been nice talking to you, Hezekiah. I'm going to go see what my *dochder* is doing," Caleb said, stepping toward the group of girls. He glanced at Irene and nodded. *"Frehlicher Grischtdaag."* He then stepped over to Susie. "What are you girls up to?"

Susie gestured toward the game. "It's Scrabble, *Dat.* Naomi gave it to me for Christmas."

"Want to play, *Onkel* Caleb?" Janie asked while putting letters on the letter stand.

"No, *danki*." Caleb nodded toward the door. "Have you seen Naomi?"

"No." Linda shook her head.

"She left a long time ago," Susie said.

"She left?" he asked.

"Ya, that's right," Susie said.

"A long time ago?" Caleb asked, glancing at the clock on the bookshelf. Could it really be close to seven? Disappointment coursed through him. How had he managed to miss Naomi? She was the one person he was truly looking forward to seeing tonight.

"Ya," Susie said. "She wasn't feeling well." She stood. "But she left me something to give you." Taking his hand, Susie pulled him toward the door. "Come upstairs with me." She glanced at her cousins. "Don't start the game without me. I'll be right back."

Susie and Caleb walked through the family room, and Caleb was surprised to see that nearly everyone had left. As he started up the stairs behind Susie, Lilly approached him.

"*Frehlicher Grischtdaag*," she said with a smile.

"Same to you," Caleb said with a nod. "Susie told me Naomi wasn't feeling well. I'm sorry that she left."

Lilly frowned. "*Ya*. It came on suddenly, and she said she had to leave. I tried to encourage her to stay, but she was determined to go."

Caleb pursed his lips. A feeling of suspicion rained down on him. Why would Naomi leave without speaking with him? Could she have been upset with him, and if so, why?

"Lilly," Miriam called, stepping into the family room. "Are you ready to go? Timothy said the snow looks pretty bad out there. We should get on the road." She looked toward the stairs. "Hi, Caleb. *Frehlicher Grischtdaag.*"

"Merry Christmas to you too, Miriam," Caleb said with a nod before trotting up the stairs after Susie. He found her in her room sitting on the bed while holding a large bag.

"This is for you from Naomi." She held it up. "Open it! It's very heavy. I can't wait to see what it is."

He opened the bag and his eyes rounded as he pulled out the antique drill he'd shown her at the flea market on Wednesday.

"Oh, Naomi," he whispered. She'd gone back and bought him exactly what he'd wanted. He examined the antique drill, and his heart filled with warmth for the beautiful, soft-spoken young woman. A small piece of paper fell into his lap, and he read the words written with a flourish:

Dear Caleb,
Please accept this small gift as a token of our new friendship. I'm so glad that God saw fit to bring you and

*Susie into my life. I look forward to sharing the holidays
with you and Susie, and I pray that with God's blessings
we'll share many more together.*

Frehlicher Grischtdaag!

Your new friend,
Naomi

Caleb stared at the note, reading it over and over again,
committing it to memory. The note touched him deep in his
soul, awakening feelings he thought he'd never feel again. He
wondered why Naomi hadn't given this gift to him in person.
Why would she write such a sweet, loving note and then give
it to Susie to deliver?

Leaning over, Susie gave him a confused expression. "*Was
iss letz?*"

"What did Naomi say when she gave you this bag?" he
asked.

Susie shrugged. "She said she didn't feel well, and she
asked me to give it to you."

"How was she acting when she gave you the bag?"

Susie shook her head. "I don't know. Upset, I guess."

"Upset?" He let the word roll through his mind as he tried
to remember when he saw her. He'd been trapped in the sitting room listening to Hezekiah's monologue when he spotted Naomi chatting with and hugging Susie. He remembered
thinking that Naomi looked like an angel as she smiled and
spoke to his daughter. His heart had swelled when he ob-
served the two of them talking together. Naomi was like no
woman he'd met since he'd lost Barbara. He could tell that
Naomi truly loved Susie, and Susie loved her as well.

And Caleb loved Naomi.

He shook his head at the realization. Yes, he did love her, and he needed to know why she'd left in such a rush. If she'd been ill, he would've been happy to take her home. Why did she rush out without even saying hello to him? Maybe there was something that had upset her. If Susie had been the last person to see her, maybe she would hold the key to finding out what had upset Naomi.

He turned to his daughter. "Did you say anything to Naomi before she left?"

Susie looked at him like he was crazy. "*Ya*. I said good-bye."

He shook his head. "No, that's not what I meant. Did you say anything that might have upset her?"

She shook her head. "I don't think so."

"Please, Susie." He placed his hand on her shoulder. "Can you try to think about everything you and Naomi discussed before she left?"

Deep in thought, she tapped her chin and looked up at the ceiling. "We talked about Christmas gifts. I gave her the little doll I bought her, and she gave me the game and a *schee* quilt that I love." She tapped a pretty quilt on her bed. "Then I asked her to play the game with me, and she said that she would play it with me every time I came to visit. So I told her we were moving here, and she was really surprised."

"You told her?" He'd hoped that he could get a chance to speak with her alone and tell Naomi the news, but he wasn't surprised that Susie was excited to share it, especially with Naomi.

However, Caleb had hoped that the news would be something he and Naomi could celebrate. Why would that news cause her to leave without speaking to him? Had he been wrong about her feelings for him?

He studied his daughter's eyes, praying she held the key to what had upset Naomi. "What exactly did you tell her?"

Susie shrugged again. "I don't know. I said that you'd found us a house and that *Aenti* Sadie said you might work for Irene's *dat*."

"You told her that I'd be working with Hezekiah?"

"No, I said I didn't know." Looking confused, she hugged the blanket to her chest. "I said that *Aenti* Sadie said you might. I mentioned that I didn't think Irene liked me because she's not nice to me and she didn't want me to come to dinner with you and her. I also told her that I have a hard time using my manners when she's around and that Irene acted like she only wanted to be alone with you. I said that I could never be friends with Irene, but I was friends with Naomi." She paused, blushing a little. "And I also said that I wanted you to be with Naomi and not with Irene."

Caleb frowned. *This is not good.* "What did Naomi say?"

"She kind of looked sad," Susie said.

Caleb stood and placed the drill on the bureau while he considered Susie's story. It didn't make sense. Was Naomi upset that Caleb might be working with Hezekiah? But why would that upset her—unless it had something to do with Irene? Was she jealous of Irene? Did she feel the same strong attraction to Caleb that he felt for her? If so, then being jealous of Irene might make sense—except that nothing was going on between him and Irene.

"Oh, there you are," Sadie said, stepping into the room.

"The girls are cleaning up the kitchen, Susie." Her eyes moved to the bureau. "What's that?"

"It's a Christmas gift from a friend," Caleb said, lifting up the drill and stepping toward the door. "Susan, please go down and help your cousins in the kitchen."

"Okay." Susie hopped down from the bed and skipped out of the room.

"What is it?" Sadie asked, her nose scrunched as she studied the drill.

"It's an antique drill," he said, holding the note from Naomi in his hand. He stuck it in his pocket for safe keeping.

"Oh." She smiled and clasped her hands together. "I saw you talking to Hezekiah and Irene. Have you decided to go into business with him?"

Caleb frowned. "No, I haven't. I've already told you what my plans are, and I need you to respect them. I'm tired of repeating myself over and over again, Sadie."

She blanched. "Well, it was *gut* to see you talking to Irene again. I think she would be a good *maedel* for you. I think she likes you."

He ran a hand down his chin and considered his response as his blood boiled with frustration. "I don't know how else to say this to you since you refuse to listen. Therefore, I'm going to say it the only way I know how. Sadie, I need you to mind your own business. I'm going to make the best decisions I can make for my *dochder* and me, and I need you to worry about your own family."

She winced. "Caleb, I only want what's best for you. It's my job to watch out for you since *Mamm* and *Dat* are gone."

He shook his head. "I'm a grown man, Sadie. Let me live my life the way I choose to live it." He held up the drill. "This gift is from a very special friend."

She raised her eyebrows, looking curious. "Who is this special friend?"

"Naomi King," he said with a smile. "That's who I—"

"Caleb!" A voice shouted from downstairs. "Caleb, come quick!"

Dropping the drill on the bed, Caleb rushed down the stairs, taking them two at a time, to where Robert stood next to Elam and Titus King, who were both frowning while holding their snowy hats.

"*Was iss letz?*" Caleb asked, his heart pounding in his chest as he looked between Elam and Robert.

"Naomi's missing," Elam said.

"What?" Caleb asked. "What do you mean?"

"She never made it home." Titus shook his head. "Lilly told Elam that Naomi didn't feel well and walked home alone, but she wasn't there when we arrived. We've searched our road and the surrounding area, but we haven't seen any sign of her."

"We need to look for her," Robert said, grabbing his coat from the peg by the door. "I'll get my horse hitched to my buggy."

"What's going on?" Sadie asked.

"Naomi's missing," Caleb said, putting on his hat and gloves. "We're going to go look for her." He grabbed a flashlight from the table by the door.

Sadie gasped. "Oh, no."

Caleb followed Elam and Robert to the door. He turned around one last time and faced Sadie. "Tell Susie I'll be home soon."

CHAPTER 15

Which way do you think she went?" Caleb asked Elam as they stood by Elam's buggy in the driveway. The snow blew so hard that Caleb shivered and wiped the flakes from his face.

Elam shook his head. "I don't know. I thought she would've taken the main roads, but maybe she didn't."

Caleb turned in the direction of the pasture and remembered how he'd stood on the porch the night before and thought about how he could walk to her house. "Maybe she thought she'd take a shortcut?"

"Maybe," Elam said.

"I'll walk around the pasture, and you two go in the buggy and check the main roads again," Caleb said, holding up the flashlight, which gave a soft yellow glow reflecting off the snow. "Tell Robert to take his buggy further up the road past your house in case she made a wrong turn."

"Sounds *gut*." Titus walked up to them. "I remember one time when Naomi was a teenager, she was out in a blizzard getting medicine and the buggy broke down not far from here. One of the wheels came clear off the hub." He gestured in the direction of the pasture. "She walked home and she may have gone through this pasture."

"Oh no," Caleb said. "She's done this before?"

Titus nodded. "*Ya*. She made it home okay that time, but I'm not certain the wind was blowing like it is tonight."

Caleb shook his head as dread pooled in his gut. "I pray she's not hurt."

"I know." Titus looked grim. "Maybe you can find her footprints in the snow. Be careful."

"You too." Caleb set out across the pasture, his boots crunching as he trudged through the deep snow. He silently sent up prayers, begging God to lead him to Naomi. He hoped and prayed she was okay.

While he walked, he thought about her note in his pocket. Naomi had to be okay. They could have a future together, as a family, with Susie.

He couldn't imagine losing her. He'd just met her, and she already meant so much to him.

Losing another person he cared about would simply be too much ...

As he moved through the snow, he lost his footing and nearly slipped. He righted himself again and then moved forward.

As he crossed the pasture the visibility worsened, and he couldn't see the house behind him or the fence in front of him. Lifting the flashlight, he searched the surrounding snow, looking for footprints. He thought again of Titus's story about Naomi walking home in a blizzard and he wondered if she'd taken this path. Was that why she thought she could make it home alone in this fierce storm?

Caleb spotted faint tracks that he thought might be her

footprints, and he followed them, moving slowly despite the frigid wind. "Naomi?" he called. "Naomi, are you out there?"

He trudged forward, following the tracks and shouting her name. Holding the flashlight up higher, he silently begged God to lead him to her. He needed to find her. He needed her in his life. Caleb continued on, marching through the snow and praying while he moved the flashlight back and forth and searched for any sign of her.

Suddenly, off in the distance, he thought he spotted something in the snow. Tenting his hand over his eyes, he tried to focus his eyes against the blowing flakes. The object looked like a black blanket peppered with snow.

Could that be her cloak?

His heart pounded against his rib cage as he quickened his steps.

"Naomi!" he shouted. "Naomi! Are you there?" As he approached, the black blanket came into view, resembling a person lying in the snow.

"Naomi?" he called, nearly running through the snow. "Is that you, Naomi?"

His heart beat faster when she didn't respond. Anxiety shot through him. *She's hurt!*

Caleb broke into a run, slipping and sliding over to the person. "Naomi?" he called. "Is that you?"

He found Naomi lying on her back with her eyes closed. Her cheeks were bright red, and her lips were a light shade of blue.

"Oh no," he moaned, praying softly. "Lord, please don't let it be too late. Don't take her from me now. Please, don't!"

Placing the flashlight in the snow, he pulled her into his

arms. "Naomi. Please answer me." When she didn't respond, panic gripped him, stealing his words for a moment. "I can't lose you, Naomi. Please answer me. Please, Naomi. I need you. Susie and I both need you." He sucked in a breath and silently prayed with all of the emotional strength he had left in him.

She moaned and stirred, causing him to release the breath he'd been holding.

"You hear me," he said. "It's okay if you can't answer. I'm going to get you home, and I'm going to take care of you." He liked the sound of that. He wanted to take care of her on a more permanent basis starting right now.

Slowly, he grabbed the flashlight and then lifted her into his arms. He heard the hum of a car and the clip-clop of hooves in the distance and he knew that he would locate the road if he followed those sounds.

Holding Naomi close to his chest, Caleb managed to balance the flashlight in one of his hands. In a hurry to get her to safety, he moved as quickly as he could while trying his best to not lose his footing in the snow. He slipped twice and slowed his pace down slightly.

He marched through the snow, praying that he would find his way to the road and Naomi would be okay. The sounds of the cars and hooves grew louder, and he knew he was heading in the right direction.

"We're almost there, Naomi," he said. "I can hear road noise up ahead of us." When she stirred again, he hoped she'd answer him. "Naomi? Are you awake? You're going to be just fine. I promise I'll take *gut* care of you."

"Caleb?" she asked, her voice tired and hoarse. "Caleb?" She looked up at him. "Where am I?"

"I found you in the pasture," he said, still trudging through the snow. "I'm so thankful I located you in this horrendous storm. Are you hurt?"

"*Ya*. I think so." She sucked in a deep breath with her face red and tears spilling from her brown eyes. "It's my ankle. I fell, and it twisted. It hurts so much." She wrapped her arms around his neck, and he relished the feeling of holding her so close.

"Don't worry," he said. "We're almost there. I promise I'll get you home safe."

"*Danki*." She rested her head on his shoulder.

Caleb felt a weight lift from his shoulders. He was thankful that she was awake and talking. Now he just had to get her home into the warmth and then have someone look at her ankle. She was lucky that only her ankle was hurt. A twinge of frustration nipped at him as he considered how much worse this situation could've turned out.

"What were you thinking trying to walk home alone in these conditions?" he asked.

"I thought I'd be okay," she said, holding tight to his neck. "I thought I could find my way. I've done it once before, and I found my house despite the snow."

"I don't think that would be possible in this blizzard." He spotted the fence in front of them. Relief flooded him. If they were close to the fence that meant they were almost to the road! "You're lucky I found you. You could've been out there all night and wound up with pneumonia or worse."

"I know," she said with a sigh. "It wasn't very smart."

Although the questions of why she left were still haunting him, Caleb carried her in silence while he concentrated on balancing her and the flashlight in his arms and continuing their trek through the blowing snow. She shivered against him, and he wished he had a blanket to shield her against the frigid weather.

When he stepped onto the road he spotted a buggy bouncing toward them with lanterns blazing like a beacon. "I hope this is Elam," he said, picking up his pace.

The buggy approached, and Titus jumped out. "Naomi!" he called. "You found her!" He trotted over and took Naomi from his arms. "What were you thinking, *dochder*? You scared us to death."

"I'm sorry, *Dat*," she said, her voice breaking into a sob.

Caleb hugged his arms to his chest. He could only imagine the fear Titus and Irma had felt for their daughter. He'd felt the same terror when he thought he'd lost Susie at the farmers market.

Titus looked at Caleb. "*Danki*."

Caleb nodded. "*Gern gschehne*."

Titus looked down at Naomi. "Let's get you home where it's warm and dry."

Caleb sat in Naomi's family room while he awaited the news on her injuries. Titus had carried her into her bedroom where her mother was going to examine her ankle and help her change into dry clothes. He'd spent the time drinking cocoa and talking with her siblings, but his mind had been focused on her, worrying and thinking of what he'd say when he finally got to talk to her again.

"Caleb," Irma called. "Naomi would like to see you."

He made his way to the bedroom located behind the kitchen and stood in the doorway.

Naomi gave a forced smile while she lay propped up on the bed with pillows. A quilt covered the length of her, and only her foot, wrapped in bandages, and the white sleeves of her nightgown were visible. Her cheeks and nose were still pink from the cold. She sipped from a mug of cocoa and then motioned for him to come in.

"I'll be right outside the door," Irma said as she stepped past Caleb.

"How are you feeling?" Caleb asked, moving to the end of the bed.

"I've been better," Naomi said. "The *gut* news is it's not broken." She nodded toward her foot. "It's a few pretty shades of red, but my *mamm* thinks it's just a real bad sprain. I was really cold, but there's no sign of frostbite. Cocoa helped warm me up right away."

"You're very lucky," Caleb said, sinking into a chair. "Everyone was worried about you. Robert was out looking in his buggy too. I'm glad I found you."

"I am too." She nodded. "*Danki.*"

"You're welcome." He smiled and then wagged a finger at her with feigned anger. "Don't you ever scare me like that again."

She laughed, revealing her adorable dimple. "I'll try not to."

"Now, tell me," he began, leaning against the bedpost, "why did you rush out of the party after you gave Susie her gifts?" He was certain her cheeks turned a deeper shade of pink.

"I didn't feel well," she said, fingering the ties on her prayer covering.

He raised an eyebrow with disbelief. "Then why didn't you ask Elam or me to take you home?"

She shrugged. "I didn't want to take anyone away from the party."

He snorted. "I would've been *froh* for you to steal me away from Hezekiah Wagler. That man held me captive with his boring stories for hours."

Naomi chuckled. "Did he?"

"I thought he would never stop talking." He raked his hand through his hair. "Why didn't you look for me?"

She frowned. "I'd thought you were busy with Hezekiah and Irene."

"Busy?"

"Talking business." She lifted her mug and took another sip.

He shook his head. "No, we weren't."

She gave him a thoughtful expression.

"*Danki* for the gift," he said. "It's perfect."

She cleared her throat. "*Gern gschehne.*"

He took a deep breath. It was time for him to be honest about his feelings. He pulled her note from his pocket. "I was touched to get this. It meant a lot to me."

Her cheeks flushed a deeper pink. "I'm glad to hear that."

"I wanted to tell you that I—" he began.

"I think it's time for you to get some rest, Naomi," Irma interrupted, stepping into the room. "It's very late and tomorrow is Christmas." She tapped Caleb's shoulder. "Robert is here. He stopped by to see if we'd found you. He's ready to take you home."

"Okay." Caleb stood. "Let me just say good-bye."

Irma gave him a stern expression. "Keep it short."

Feeling like a teenager, Caleb nodded and suppressed a grin. Did Irma truly think he was planning on misbehaving with her injured daughter?

Caleb waited until Irma stepped out to the kitchen and then walked around the bed to Naomi. Taking her hand in his, he looked deep into her eyes, which rounded with surprise.

"I'm glad you're okay," he said softly. "I was very worried about you."

She nodded, looking speechless.

"*Danki* again for the note you gave me with the drill," he said, holding the note up before putting it back into his pocket. "Your words touched me deeply. I, too, am looking forward to where our friendship takes us." He shook her hand. "*Frehlicher Grischtdaag, mei freind.*"

"*Frehlicher Grischtdaag,*" she echoed, her eyes still wide.

He then stepped out into the kitchen. "*Gut nacht,*" he said to Irma.

"*Danki*, Caleb," Irma said, shaking his hand. "We're so glad you rescued her."

❦

Naomi adjusted herself in the bed. The pain from her ankle radiated up her leg in waves, stealing her breath.

However, the buzz in her mind affected her more deeply than the pain from her foot as she watched Caleb walk out into the kitchen. Her heart pounded and a smile spread on her lips as she remembered the look on his face as he'd held her hand. His words had left her both dizzy and speechless.

The note she'd written to him had touched him, and he looked forward to a future with her.

A future?

But what did that mean exactly? Did he only want to be friends or did he want something more?

"You're a very blessed *maedel*," Irma said, stepping back into the bedroom. "You could've been lost out there all night."

Naomi sighed. "I know." She tried to move her leg and sucked in a ragged breath when the discomfort shot through her ankle.

"*Ach*," her mother rushed over and took her hand. "Are you okay?"

Naomi nodded as the pain subsided a bit. "I think so."

"Do you want more painkiller?" Her mother's eyes were wide with worry.

"No, *danki*." Naomi forced a smile. "I'll be okay in a moment. The pain comes and goes."

Her mother pulled a chair up next to her. "Caleb is a *gut* man."

Naomi blinked, stunned by how direct her mother was.

Irma smiled. "I believe he may have feelings for you."

Naomi cleared her throat. "I'm not certain about that, but I hope so."

Irma raised an eyebrow. "I believe you know the answer to that."

Shaking her head, Naomi smoothed the quilt over her nightgown. "Susie told me that Caleb found a house and they're moving here, but I'm not certain of what that will mean for him and me. All I know is that I do care for him and Susie, and I hope to get to know them better."

"He cares for you too, Naomi," Irma said with a knowing smile. "I believe he cares quite deeply for you. I wish you could've seen his face when your *dat* carried you in."

Naomi rubbed the back of her neck, which was stiff from the fall. "I don't understand."

Irma rubbed Naomi's arm. "He was worried sick about you. I was wrong to tell you not to consider him because he's a widower." She smiled. "My mother's favorite verse was from Romans. It went something like this: 'But if we hope for what we do not yet have, we wait for it patiently.'"

Naomi shook her head. "What are you trying to say, *Mamm*?"

"You've waited for your true love," Irma said, still smiling. "Now let God lead you and Caleb down the road."

"My true love?" Naomi whispered.

"I think so, but only time will tell. See where God leads you and Caleb. I think you're off to a *gut* start." Irma stood. "You need to get some sleep."

"What about the Christmas table?"

Irma kissed Naomi's head. "I'll take care of it."

"*Danki*," Naomi said, trying to find a comfortable position on the bed despite the discomfort in her ankle.

"You get better." Irma wagged a finger at her. "And don't you ever take off alone in the snow again. You hear me?"

Naomi smiled. "Yes, *Mamm*. I definitely learned my lesson. *Gut nacht*."

"*Gut nacht*." Her mother left, gently closing the door behind her.

Naomi stared up at the ceiling, ignoring her injury and

thinking of Caleb. She fell asleep with a smile on her face, dreaming of her possible future with Caleb and Susie.

Epilogue

Naomi smiled despite the pain in her ankle while sitting at the kitchen table the following afternoon. Around her, all of her siblings laughed, ate candy, and played with their new toys.

"Naomi," her father said, tapping her on the shoulder. "You have visitors."

"I do?" She looked up at him, hoping that her prayers had come true. She'd been thinking of Caleb and Susie all morning.

"Let me help you into the *schtupp*." Taking her arm, Titus helped Naomi while she half hopped, half limped.

Moving to the doorway, she found Caleb and Susie standing in the room, and tears filled Naomi's eyes. Her prayers had been answered. She was going to spend Christmas with her new friends.

Caleb rushed over and took Naomi's other arm. "Let me help you."

"*Danki*," Naomi said, her cheeks burning with embarrassment.

"Are you in much pain?" he asked, his green eyes filling with concern.

"I'll be fine," she said.

They helped her to the sofa, and she sank onto the end cushion.

Susie rushed over and hugged Naomi. "*Frehlicher Grischtdaag!*"

"*Frehlicher Grischtdaag, mei liewe,*" Naomi said before kissing the little girl's head.

"Can I go see Levina and Sylvia?" Susie asked.

"Of course," Naomi said, gesturing toward the adjacent room. "Have fun."

Susie ran off toward the kitchen.

The sofa shifted beside Naomi as Caleb lowered himself down next to her. "*Frehlicher Grischtdaag.*" He handed her a bag.

"Oh, Caleb," Naomi said, taking the bag. "You didn't have to."

He laughed. "Of course I did. Please open it."

Naomi's heart fluttered as she opened the bag and pulled out the black Bible she'd longed to buy for herself. She ran her fingers over the cover. "Caleb," she whispered, meeting his intense stare. "You spent too much."

"No, I didn't." He nodded toward the Bible. "Please open it. There's something inside."

She opened the cover and found a note in neat handwriting:

Naomi,

I thought it was only fitting to give you this Bible for Christmas. I know how much it would mean to you to have a new Bible for your nightly devotions. I hope that you realize how much you mean to both Susie and me.

*Your friendship is precious to us, just like the precious
verses contained in this holy book.*

*I'm so thankful that God led Susie and me back to
my hometown for Christmas and I'm even more thankful
that He led me to you. You've taught me so much about
finding joy in life again despite past heartaches. You've
helped me remember what it means to be happy. I look
forward to where God leads us on this journey together.*

Frehlicher Grischtdaag!
Caleb

She read the words over and over again, and she was both
stunned and confused by the sentiment they contained.
Questions swirled in her mind. She needed to know what
the inscription truly meant, but she couldn't form the words
to ask him.

Finally, with tears pooling in her eyes, Naomi looked up.
"*Danki.* It's *schee.*"

He touched her hand, and her pulse skittered. "I need to
know something. What did you mean last night when you
said you thought I was discussing business with Hezekiah
and Irene?"

"Susie said you were going into business with Hezekiah,"
Naomi said.

Caleb shook his head. "No, I'm not. I found a house that
has a shop, and I'm going to open my own carriage shop."

Naomi smiled. "That's *wunderbaar!*"

"Hezekiah and Irene were talking my ear off last night,
but it was nothing but idle conversation."

Naomi took a deep breath and glanced down at the Bible.

She needed to know the truth about him and Irene. "Are you courting Irene?" she asked while running her fingers over the cover of the Bible.

He snorted. "No. Why do you ask?"

She met his expression, not finding any sign of a lie. "I heard Sadie talking."

He frowned. "What did *mei schweschder* say now?"

"She was telling someone that you and Irene would be a *gut* couple. She made a point of saying that Susie needed a *mamm*, implying that Irene could be a *gut* candidate for that role."

Caleb rolled his eyes. "Sadie tries too hard to run my life. She means well, but she does more damage than good." His frown deepened. "And the last role that Irene would be *gut* for would be a *mamm*. She's terrible with Susie, and she's been nothing but rude to my precious *dochder*."

Naomi shook her head. "I can't imagine ever being rude or nasty to Susie. She's such a special girl. I'm sorry that Irene isn't nice to Susie, but I'm so glad Sadie was wrong."

"Sadie has been wrong about a lot of things," Caleb said. "Most of all, she was wrong about who I belong with. I definitely don't belong with Irene."

"Is that so?" Naomi's smile reappeared.

He nodded, his own smile growing. "She's not any fun to go shopping with."

"And I would imagine she doesn't like root beer." Naomi coyly tapped her chin. "I seem to remember that you promised me a root beer float."

He grinned. "I did. And I intend to keep that promise." His smile faded. "But I must ask you one question first."

"What's that?"

He took her hands in his, and the feel of his warm skin caused her heart to beat at hyper speed. "Naomi, that time we sat on the porch together, you asked me if I believed God gave second chances at true love. I told you yes, but I honestly wasn't sure." His eyes sparkled. "Since I've met you, I know that answer for certain. I think God has given me a second chance when he brought me to you. We would be a *gut* couple, and I would be honored to court you."

Tears filled her eyes. "After I had my heart broken twice, I was certain I'd never find love. Now I see that God had a plan all along for me. I think this is the Christmas miracle Susie wanted for you. It's also a miracle for me."

"She told me that she'd asked you if you believed in miracles," he said, running his finger down her jaw line.

She nodded, butterflies fluttering in her belly at the feel of his gentle touch.

"She also asked me if I believe in miracles, and I do believe in them," he said. "And, *ya*, my little girl was right because you're my miracle. No, actually, you're a miracle for Susie and me. We both love you." He nodded toward the Bible. "There's a reason why I didn't have your name engraved on the Bible. I thought that you might change your name someday and I wanted to be certain that I put the correct name on the cover."

Before she could respond, he leaned over and gently pressed his lips against hers, sending the pit of her stomach into a wild swirl.

"*Frehlicher Grischtdaag*, Naomi," he whispered against her lips.

"*Frehlicher Grischtdaag,*" she whispered, leaning her head against his shoulder and closing her eyes.

RASPBERRY DREAM TORTE

1-10 oz. pkg. frozen raspberries
1¼ cup vanilla wafer crumbs
¼ cup melted butter
½ cup butter
1½ cups 10x (confectioner's) sugar
¼ t. vanilla
¼ t. almond extract
¼ cup sugar
2 T. cornstarch
Whipped cream for garnish
2 eggs

Defrost raspberries. Combine vanilla wafer crumbs and ¼ cup melted butter. Press into bottom of 7 ½-inch spring form pan. Cream ½ cup butter and 10x sugar. Add eggs, beating well after each. Blend in extracts. Spread over crumb layer. Chill until firm. Combine sugar, cornstarch, and raspberries in a pan. Cook on stovetop at medium heat, stirring constantly until clear and thick. Pour raspberry filling over torte. Refrigerate several hours. Garnish with whipped cream.

Discussion Questions

1. At the beginning of the story, Naomi feels that she's lost her chance to find true love. She thinks that after two failed relationships, God is telling her that she's meant to be her mother's helper instead of a wife. Have you ever felt as if God has given up on you, and you've lost your chance at happiness? Were your feelings validated or did your experience change for the better? Share this with the group.

2. Naomi's mother quotes 2 Corinthians 1:7, "And our hope for you is firm, because we know that just as you share in our sufferings, so also you share in our comfort." What does this verse mean to you?

3. Sadie thinks she is helping Caleb by offering constant unsolicited advice, even though he frequently asks her to mind her own business. Think of a time when you may have had misguided intentions for a child or loved one. Share this with the group.

4. At the end of the story, Caleb and Naomi believe that their love is a Christmas miracle and God is giving them both a second chance at happiness. Have you ever experienced a second chance or a Christmas miracle? Share this with the group.

5. Which character can you identify with the most? Which character seemed to carry the most emotional stake in the story?

6. How does Naomi grow and change throughout the story?

7. Gossip, even in a community that is supposed to be Christlike, can hurt and lead to misunderstanding. Do we do this in our own church communities—judge and gossip about our fellow Christians without considering the consequences? How does this impact the community?

8. Susie wants a real family and is willing to give up her life in Ohio for her life in Lancaster. Have you ever moved, giving up everything you've ever known with blind faith? Do you think it was God calling you to do something different?

9. How does Naomi's friendship with Lilly guide Naomi on her journey to accepting her love for Caleb? How does Naomi's mother impact the journey? What role does Susie play?

10. Although Irene is interested in Caleb, he does not want to court her since she doesn't attempt to establish a relationship with Susie. Have you ever limited a friendship because all parties involved were not equally interested?

11. What did you learn about Amish holiday traditions? What is your opinion of their customs? Should we, as

non-Amish, adopt more of their traditions of making Christmas more religious and less commercial? Share your thoughts with the group.

Acknowledgments

I'm thankful to my loving and supportive family, including my mother, Lola Goebelbecker; my husband, Joe; my sons, Zac and Matt; my mother-in-law, Sharon Clipston; and my wonderful aunts, Trudy Janitz and Debbie Floyd.

I'm more grateful than words can express for my amazing friends who critique and edit for me: Jean Love, Sue McKlveen, and Lauran Rodriguez. Special thanks to Lauran for admiring the character of Naomi King and inspiring this book.

Thank you also to Ruth Meily for her continued help with Lancaster County research and recipes. I'm also grateful to Cathy Zimmermann for her help and quick answers to my Amish and Lancaster County questions. Thank you also to Stacey Barbalace for her help with the Amish details and accuracy.

As always, thank you to my special Amish friend who patiently answers my endless stream of questions.

Thank you to my awesome agent, Mary Sue Seymour, for her professional expertise and her friendship.

I'm grateful for the fabulous team at Zondervan, especially Sue Brower, Becky Philpott, and Alicia Mey.

Thank you also to my faithful readers for your love and friendship.

Thank you most of all, God, for giving me the opportunity to glorify You. I'm so thankful and humbled You've chosen this path for me.

Special thanks to Cathy and Dennis Zimmermann for their hospitality and research assistance in Lancaster County, Pennsylvania.

Cathy & Dennis Zimmermann, Innkeepers
The Creekside Inn
44 Leacock Road—PO Box 435
Paradise, PA 17562
Toll Free: (866) 604–2574
Local Phone: (717) 687–0333

The author and publisher gratefully acknowledge the following resources that were used to research information for this book:

C. Richard Beam, *Revised Pennsylvania German Dictionary: English to Pennsylvania Dutch* (Brookshire Publications, 1991).

Rose Heiberger, *Buggy Seat Bare Feet*, rev. ed. (Gordonville, Pennsylvania Print Shop, 1994).

A Plain and Simple Christmas

A Novella

Amy Clipston

Take a trip to Bird-in-Hand, Pennsylvania, where you'll meet the women of the Kauffman Amish Bakery in Lancaster County. As each woman's story unfolds, you will share in her heartaches, trials, joys, dreams ... and secrets. You'll discover how the simplicity of the Amish lifestyle can clash with the "English" way of life—and the decisions and consequences that follow. Most importantly, you will be encouraged by the hope and faith of these women, and the importance they place on their families.

In the tradition of her widely popular Kauffman Amish Bakery Series, author Amy Clipston tells the tale of Anna Mae McDonough who was shunned by her family four years ago when she left her Amish community in Lancaster County, PA, to marry an "Englisher" and move with him to Baltimore. Now, eight months pregnant with her first child, she longs to return home for Christmas to reconcile with her family, especially her stern father, who is the religious leader for her former Amish church district.

So Anna Mae writes a letter to Kathryn Beiler, her brother's wife, to enlist her help. Kathryn asks her husband, David, if she should arrange Anna Mae's visit. David cautions her that a visit would cause too much stress in the family and instead suggests they visit Anna Mae and her husband in the spring. However, Kathryn arranges the visit anyway, believing in her heart that it's God's will for the family to heal.

When Anna Mae arrives in Lancaster for Christmas, the welcome she receives is nothing like what she had hoped for.

A book filled with love, the pain of being separated from one's family, and the determination to follow God's will regardless of the outcome, *A Plain and Simple Christmas* is an inspiring page-turner that will keep you guessing what happens next ... right to the very last page.

Kauffman Amish Bakery Series

A Gift of Grace

A Novel

Amy Clipston

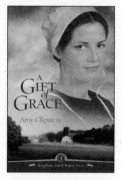

Rebecca Kauffman's tranquil Old Order Amish life is transformed when she suddenly has custody of her two teenage nieces after her English sister and brother-in-law are killed in an automobile accident. Instant motherhood, after years of unsuccessful attempts to conceive a child of her own, is both a joy and a heartache. Rebecca struggles to give the teenage girls the guidance they need as well as fulfill her duties to Daniel as an Amish wife.

Rebellious Jessica is resistant to Amish ways and constantly in trouble with the community. Younger sister Lindsay is caught in the middle, and the strain between Rebecca and Daniel mounts as Jessica's rebellion escalates. Instead of the beautiful family life she dreamed of creating for her nieces, Rebecca feels as if her world is being torn apart by two different cultures, leaving her to question her place in the Amish community, her marriage, and her faith in God.

Available in stores and online!

ZONDERVAN®
.com

A Promise of Hope

A Novel

Amy Clipston

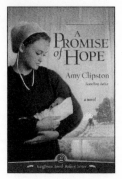

In *A Promise of Hope*, the second installment in the Kauffman Amish Bakery Series, bestselling author Amy Clipston compellingly unfolds the tensions, loves, and faith of the inhabitants of an Amish community and the family bakery that serves as an anchor point for the series.

When Sarah Troyer tragically loses her husband, Peter, she is left to raise infant twins alone. Overwhelmed and grieving, she lives with her parents in the Amish community of Bird-in-Hand, Pennsylvania. Sarah is taken completely by surprise when a stranger arrives claiming connections to Peter's past — Peter had told her he was an orphan with no family. From Luke, she learns her husband hid a secret life, one with ramifications that will change her own.

Sarah's family, concerned for her and the future of her twins, encourages her to marry again. It should make sense ... but Sarah's heart says no. She feels trapped. Should she marry a man she doesn't love? Or discover if her growing interest in Luke can be trusted?

A Promise of Hope is filled with surprising twists that will grip you to the very last words.

Available in stores and online!

Kauffman Amish Bakery Series

A Place of Peace
A Novel

Amy Clipston,
Bestselling Author of A Gift of Grace

Take a trip to Bird-in-Hand, Pennsylvania, where you'll meet the women of the Kauffman Amish Bakery in Lancaster County. As each woman's story unfolds, you will share in her heartaches, trials, joys, dreams ... and secrets. You'll discover how the simplicity of the Amish lifestyle can clash with the "English" way of life—and the decisions and consequences that follow. Most importantly, you will be encouraged by the hope and faith of these women, and the importance they place on their families.

Miriam Lapp, who left the Amish community of Bird-in-Hand three years ago, is heartbroken when her sister calls to reveal that her mother has died suddenly. Traveling home to Pennsylvania, she is forced to face the heartache from her past, including her rift from her family and the breakup of her engagement with Timothy Kauffman.

Her past emotional wounds are reopened when her family rejects her once again and she finds out that Timothy is in a relationship with someone else. Miriam discovers that the rumors that broke them up three years ago were all lies. However, when Timothy proposes to his girlfriend and Miriam's father disowns her, Miriam returns to Indiana with her heart in shambles.

When Miriam's father has a stroke, Miriam returns to Pennsylvania, where her world continues to fall apart, leaving her to question her place in the Amish community and her faith in God.

Kauffman Amish Bakery Series

A Life of Joy

Amy Clipston,
Bestselling Author of A Gift of Grace

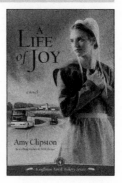

Take a trip to Bird-in-Hand, Pennsylvania, where you'll meet the women of the Kauffman Amish Bakery in Lancaster County. As each woman's story unfolds, you will share in her heartaches, trials, joys, dreams ... and secrets. You'll discover how the simplicity of the Amish lifestyle can clash with the "English" way of life — and the decisions and consequences that follow. Most importantly, you will be encouraged by the hope and faith of these women, and the importance they place on their families.

In *A Life of Joy*, the fourth installment in the series, eighteen-year-old Lindsay Bedford has reached a crossroads. Should she stay in the small Amish community she's known and loved for four years or return to the English life in her hometown in Virginia where her older sister is a college student? An extended visit to Virginia might just tip the scales as Lindsay reconnects with friends, joins a new church, works on her GED, and is pressured by her sister to stay and "make something of herself."

Will Lindsay leave her aunt Rebecca and become English or settle in Bird-in-Hand and join the Amish church? Legions of Clipston fans want to know.

Full of well-researched Amish culture, Clipston's book is true to form, delivering the best of the Amish fiction genre wrapped around a compelling story, with characters who will touch the hearts of loyal fans and new readers alike.

Coming February 2012!

Roadside Assistance

Amy Clipston

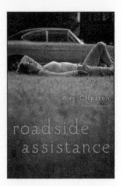

A very bumpy ride.

Emily Curtis is used to dealing with her problems while under the hood of an old Chevy, but when her mom dies, Emily's world seems shaken beyond repair. Driven from home by hospital bills they can't pay, Emily and her dad move in with his wealthy sister, who intends to make her niece more feminine—in other words, just like Whitney, Emily's perfect cousin. But when Emily hears the engine of a 1970 Dodge Challenger, and sees the cute gearhead, Zander, next door, things seem to be looking up.

But even working alongside Zander can't completely fix the hole in Emily's life. Ever since her mom died, Emily hasn't been able to pray, and no one—not even Zander—seems to understand. But sometimes the help you need can come from the person you least expect.

Available in stores and online!

Share Your Thoughts

With the Author: Your comments will be forwarded to the author when you send them to *zauthor@zondervan.com*.

With Zondervan: Submit your review of this book by writing to *zreview@zondervan.com*.

Free Online Resources at
www.zondervan.com

Zondervan AuthorTracker: Be notified whenever your favorite authors publish new books, go on tour, or post an update about what's happening in their lives at www.zondervan.com/authortracker.

Daily Bible Verses and Devotions: Enrich your life with daily Bible verses or devotions that help you start every morning focused on God. Visit www.zondervan.com/newsletters.

Free Email Publications: Sign up for newsletters on Christian living, academic resources, church ministry, fiction, children's resources, and more. Visit www.zondervan.com/newsletters.

Zondervan Bible Search: Find and compare Bible passages in a variety of translations at www.zondervanbiblesearch.com.

Other Benefits: Register to receive online benefits like coupons and special offers, or to participate in research.

ZONDERVAN.com/
AUTHORTRACKER
follow your favorite authors